THE ART

OF

HERO WORSHIP

Mia Kerick

A NineStar Press Publication

Published by NineStar Press
P.O. Box 91792,
Albuquerque, New Mexico, 87199 USA.
www.ninestarpress.com

The Art of Hero Worship

Copyright © 2018 by Mia Kerick
Cover Art by Natasha Snow Copyright © 2018
Edited by Elizabetta McKay

This is a work of fiction. Names, characters, places, and incidents are either the product of the author's imagination or are used fictitiously. Any resemblance to actual persons living or dead, business establishments, events, or locales is entirely coincidental.

All rights reserved. No part of this publication may be reproduced in any material form, whether by printing, photocopying, scanning or otherwise without the written permission of the publisher. To request permission and all other inquiries, contact NineStar Press at the physical or web addresses above or at Contact@ninestarpress.com.

Printed in the USA
First Edition
October, 2018

Print ISBN: 978-1-949909-15-9

Also available in eBook, ISBN: 978-1-949909-07-4

Warning: This book contains sexually explicit content, which may only be suitable for mature readers, depictions of an on-page school shooting and the deaths of minor characters, children in danger, and off-page suicide.

College junior Liam Norcross is a hero. He willingly, even eagerly, risks his life to save a stranger as a murderous, deranged shooter moves methodically through the darkened theater on the Batcheldor College campus, randomly killing innocent men, women, and children.

The stranger he saves is college freshman Jason Tripp. Jase loses everything in the shooting: his girlfriend, who dies on the floor beside him, and his grip on emotional security. He struggles to regain a sense of safety in the world, finally leaving college to seek refuge in his hometown.

An inexplicable bond forms between the two men in the chaos and horror of the theater, and Liam fights to bring Jase back to the world he ran away from. When Jase returns to school, they're drawn together as soulmates, and soon Liam and Jase fall into a turbulent romantic relationship. However, the rocky path to love cannot be smoothed until Jase rescues his hero in return by delving into his shady past and solving the mystery of Liam's compulsion to be everybody's savior.

For Cody Kennedy, my voice of reason,
and a hero of so many.

Part One

April

Chapter One

POP-POP-POP...

At this point, he's in the back of the theater, and the shooting hasn't slowed down at all. Gunshots ring out steadily in the shadowy darkness...always in sets of three, letting me know where he is. I'm scared...so fucking scared...but not too scared to wonder what I did to deserve this special little slice of hell.

And I'm frozen...I can't even move enough to swallow my spit. I know what I have to do—I have to search for Ginny, but I can't since I'm frozen solid, like a leg of lamb in a walk-in freezer.

Pop-pop-pop...pop-pop-pop...

"I've been shot! Oh, sweet Jesus, I've been shot!"

Earsplitting blasts of sound—one, two, three. The gunshots have a life and a plan—*no, a mission*—all their own, to maim and kill by ripping through the flesh of everyone in this theater. I'm panting and sweating and wishing to God I knew how to pray because I'd *so* pray right now.

And as suddenly as it started, the shooting stops. *Is it over?* With the utmost caution, I exhale the breath I've been hanging on to so jealously...as if part of me fears I'll never get the chance to take another. But one more wary breath moves in and out, and I know I have to get hold of myself so I can find her. Because it's over now... yes, I think maybe it's ov—

Pop-pop-pop…

Life-sucking and blood-spattering and gurgle-inducing, evenly spaced sets of three that are becoming so *horribly* predictable. I brace myself for the impact because I just *know* the next pop is going to come with excruciating pain that explodes in my head or my back or, if I'm lucky, my ass. Or, if I'm not so lucky, in all three places, one right after another.

This isn't happening. It can't be happening.

Is nineteen too old to want my mommy?

"Get down! Get on the floor!" Somebody yells. *Too late for that warning.* I'm already flat on the floor in the narrow space between the rows of seats; my head is bleeding all over the arm it's resting on… *My left arm? My right arm? Somebody else's arm? Not so sure.* Not so sure it matters.

"Don't shoot me—please don't—"

Pop-pop-pop…

"Put the gun down! Put it do-o-own!"

Pop-pop-pop…

I belly crawl forward a few inches and reach around in search of Ginny's hand, but when I pat the floor all I can feel is a pool of blood that wasn't there the last time I checked, and then there's this cooling mound of flesh in its center.

"I don't know what to do…" These words escape on a single breath followed by a few sharp coughs from an elderly man.

Pop-pop-pop…pop-pop-pop…

Annoying cough…forever suppressed.

Right after the second round of shots, when everybody had started rushing around, all frenzied and scrambling, I'd lost track of Ginny… In fact, I'd lost track of *everything*. Maybe because it had suddenly sunk into my stunned brain that this place was now a death chamber. *My* death chamber.

It seems as if so much time has passed since the first bullet whizzed past my right ear...that for a month or a year—or for my entire lifetime—I've been waiting for the gunshots to stop. But a tiny voice inside my head suggests that I've been in this living hell for less than five minutes, at most.

Pop-pop-pop...

Right after the shooting started, but before I lost Ginny, I caught a glimpse of the gunman's silhouette against the bright stage. He'd seemed huge in his dark baggy clothing. He towered over the audience, or maybe it just seemed that way because he was pointing a long gun at us. I recognized the shooter from seeing him around campus. And when I saw his face profiled in the light—the bulging forehead, prominent nose, and receding chin—a name had sped through my brain, but soon the name was as lost to me as my girlfriend's lax hand.

Pop-pop-pop...

The gunman doesn't say a word; his weapon does the talking. And the deafening popping sounds are closer again, like the gun has something it wants to say to *me personally*...something like, "You're gonna die today, Jason."

"I'm gonna push on your back really hard, and I want you to squeeze as much of your body underneath the chairs as you can, got it?" The voice seems to come from a million miles away, but it's coming from right behind me. On top of me, really. I feel his breath on the back of my neck.

Pop-pop-pop...pop-pop-pop...

"Are we going to die?" I'm not sure if I ask this or if it comes from the lips of the little old lady who'd been sitting on the other side of Ginny at the start of the play. The old lady who told us she'd come to the Harrison Theater to see her granddaughter play Ophelia in the *Shakespeare in the Spring Performance Series*, not to die in a hail of bullets. I know that Ginny didn't ask the question, though. She's been silent since the second volley of gunshots when her head slumped over unnaturally onto my shoulder, and by instinct, I'd pulled her to the floor.

Batcheldor College's small theater has been called "an acoustic gem," and right now, it's ringing with the erratic sounds of screaming and moaning and crying and shouting and shooting. But most impressive is the resounding silence of the gunman, which speaks louder than words, or gunshots, ever could.

All in all, it's noisy and confusing and crazy...the Beatles' tune "Helter Skelter" comes to mind. This is not how I want to die. Mostly because *I don't want to die!*

The guy on my back is poking a single finger into the blood on my head, then twisting in such a way that I think he's reaching to his back...like maybe he's smearing my blood there. I'm distracted from his action by the squealing of the fire alarm, and I find my blurry mind wondering if, in addition to the problem of a crazed gunman, we also have a fire to put out.

Would I prefer my death be a result of hungry flames or a hail of bullets?

"We're gonna survive; just stay still. Completely still. 'Kay?" I feel the pressure on my back that he promised me, and even though it hurts to have my belly pushed into the metal rungs at the base of the seats in front of us, I feel strangely safe. He speaks into my ear. "Play dead, dude."

Pop-pop-pop...

No, I'm not even remotely safe. But thankfully, I play dead far better than my dog Goliath did when I tried to teach him that trick at the age of seven.

The shots are already earsplitting, and growing louder, as the shooter's heading our way. I'm so fucking scared I tremble as if I'm having a seizure, and I promised the guy lying on top of me that I'd stay still. I concentrate on taking short shallow breaths, one after another, in my effort to stop shaking. To stay frozen—the way my heart has been since I pulled Ginny to the floor and promptly let go of her hand so I could curl up into a tight fetal ball.

Somebody near me sits up, scrambles to his knees, and impulsively crawls toward the far aisle.

Pop-pop-pop...

"Bang, bang...you're dead." The voice comes from directly above me; it's blank and monotone and controlled. The snicker that follows is chilling. I want nothing more than to throw the big guy off my back and run like hell toward the double doors, but I just keep on going with the short, shallow breaths and stay as still as I've ever been in my life. The guy on top of me is totally exposed; I can't move because if I do, I'll cheat him out of his life, for sure. Which is *so* not cool when he's trying to save mine.

I smell blood. Never noticed the smell of blood before. It reminds me of Grandma's penny collection...if it got spilled onto the sticky floor of the theater. The scent of old copper is everywhere like wet pennies strewn all around me on the floor.

Pop-pop-pop...

Shooter's practically on top of us now. *Don't move... don't move...don't move...*

"Dear God, help me!" This request seems to catch the shooter's attention, and he turns around and steps away from us. I curse myself for feeling as relieved as I do.

Pop-pop-pop...

We wait and it seems like forever. We wait as voices beg and plead and pray and he shuts them up with bullets. We wait as the sound of shots moves to the front left near the exit, where I figure he's shooting at anyone who tries to get out through the double doors.

And then, for a second, it's quiet.

"Now..." The big guy whispers, but the sound seems to blast into my left ear. "We have to make our move *now*." Before I agree, the heaviness of his body lifts and I feel cold and exposed. "This is our chance to get outta here..."

His hand is attached to the back of my wrist, clutching me so hard I'll have fingerprint bruises for a week...if I live so long.

"Come on! Get up!"

"Ginny..." I whisper back. "I can't leave Ginny."

He reaches out to touch the flesh mound in the center of the pool of blood and whispers firmly, "Ginny's already gone." He releases my wrist just long enough to adjust his grip. "I worked here last year. I know how to get away. *Come on...*"

He pulls me to my knees and drags me. *Ginny.* I only think her name this time because I'm literally too petrified to speak. We crawl like two sneaky toddlers through the narrow alley between the rows of seats and then down the outside aisle, over a couple of bodies—small ones, kids' bodies that are way too still and cool—and to a trapdoor at the base of the stage. It's a small gray square in the wall. I never noticed it before, and I've been to the Harrison Theater at least five times this year to see Ginny's roommate perform. The guy beside me pulls out a pocketknife and fiddles silently with the screws holding the little door in place.

Pop-pop-pop...

The thin slab of metal covering the small door drops to the floor and contributes a new sound to the quieting chaos. It clangs in such a way that nobody left alive in the theater could miss it.

"Where do you think you're going?" The gunman has stopped shooting, and I hear the heavy stomping of combat boots coming toward us, down the aisle. Not running...just walking in swift, determined steps. My guardian angel grabs me and stuffs me through the opening in the base of the stage. I land on my chin in a pile of music stands. My helper isn't far behind in squeezing his bulky frame through the small square in the wall. We've landed in some type of a cluttered crawl space, maybe the orchestra pit, and I struggle to make my way through the music stands in the pitch-blackness. When we're halfway through the mess of metal, crawling through unruly stacks of folding chairs, the overhead light in the pit flicks on.

"What's going on in the theater, you guys? It's mega-loud in there." A clueless college girl's voice. I can't see her clearly because the sudden bright light stings my eyes, making me squint.

"Get out of here, lady—just run for it!" shouts my guardian angel. We can't run yet because we're still trapped in a dense forest of metal.

"I see you two... I see you." The shooter's voice is deadly calm. "And I think I *know* you."

Pop-pop-pop...

For some reason, he doesn't climb into the orchestra pit to come after us but pushes the gun through the opening and pulls the trigger three times. Bullets ricochet off the metal chairs and stands. Again I freeze, not sure which way to go. I'm grabbed fiercely by my right forearm and dragged over the remainder of the chairs to the door.

I expect more shooting, but there's none. Instead, that cold, creepy voice increases in volume, to assure us, "Don't worry, I'll find you."

We take to our feet and start to run. Soon we're holding hands in a narrow hallway...running for the back of the building...and then we're outside in the breezy darkness, still clinging to each other. We sprint through the muddy grass in the direction of the parking lot.

And we stop at an old model, cherry-red muscle car—a Dodge Charger.

"Get in!" His voice is husky as he opens the passenger door, pushes me inside, and quickly shuts it. Then he scrambles over the hood to get to the driver's side. He flings the door wide open and jumps into the seat, not gracefully, but with more speed than I could ever have imagined was possible for a guy his size. Adrenaline counts for a lot... And soon we're driving off the college grounds, out of the supposed safety of the "Batcheldor College Bubble," and into the real world.

Chapter Two

A COUPLE OF blocks from the theater, the big guy pulls his car over to the side of Main Street because a whole slew of screaming official law enforcement vehicles are heading toward us, in the direction of the theater.

I yell at him, "No! K-keep driving!" I'm breathing so fast I can hardly get the words out, yet I have to make this stranger understand me—we can't stop moving yet.

"We have to tell the cops what we know…and plus, your head, man…you're *covered* in blood and…" He's still driving, but he's doing it more slowly than I want, and he's peering at me every couple of seconds with wide freaked-out eyes. "I just wanna make sure you're okay and it…you know…looks like you might've got shot on the top of your head and…"

I'm dizzy as hell, and I have no idea why my head is bleeding so much. But I know one thing for sure—I can't let him stop driving now, or maybe ever. "N-n-n…" I fail at my first attempt to form a word. "P-p-p…P-p-please drive."

"'Kay, dude…" He sighs long and loud, and I look at him—I really study him—for the first time. He's well over six feet tall and rugged. His blond hair is cut in a style that stands up off the top of his head a few inches and is balanced by a long, squared-off beard that's a few shades darker than his hair. But my eyes are drawn to a smear of blood on the bridge of his nose that somehow got beneath his thick, black-rimmed glasses. The overall effect is *urban lumberjack badass who barely survived a dangerous encounter with a giant red oak.* Not that this observation makes any difference to our desperate situation.

"You know we've gotta go to the police soon...you know that, right?" His voice is deep and gruff, and he seems nervous, but then, under the circumstances, who, in his right mind, wouldn't be?

I don't respond. I actually can't because I'm going to be sick. I roll down the window and hang my head out in a feeble attempt to vomit on the street as it rolls by. I'm only half successful, and I feel bad for messing up this guy's pristine car. My head is spinning with dizzying memories of gunshots and the smell of pennies and dark images of death in a small college theater. And thoughts of Ginny...

No—I push her face from my mind because I'm not yet ready to accept what a large part of me knows to be true. "Can't we...c-can't we k-keep on driving? Can't w-we?"

The big blond guy slows the car down and examines me carefully with wide dark eyes. "You look like shit... I... uh...think you might be in shock or something." He stops the car and turns it around, and then he heads down a nearby side street. "Hey, I know a place we can go and you can get yourself together. But as soon as you're cool with everything we gotta go to the cops. We have to tell them about Dom."

"Not to th-the dorms. Not going to th-the dorms." I'm a hot mess.

"No, I don't think that would be too smart because Dom said he knows us, and he probably also knows we live in RetroHouse and...and he might decide to... *Jesus!*" The fact that we're still in serious danger hits him hard. "Not gonna let him hurt you, man."

I'm strangely warmed by my self-appointed guardian's protectiveness, but also distracted by the name

Dom...*Domenic DeSalles*. It's the name that fleetingly visited my brain earlier tonight when the slaughter started. And, yeah, there's a pretty good chance that Domenic DeSalles will come to our dorm rooms to kill us in our sleep. To finish the job he started in the theater by blowing our brains out with his AR-15.

"I'm taking care of a friend's cat because he's on a job interview in Boston this weekend. He'd be cool with us crashing at his apartment until we figure out which end is up."

EVEN THOUGH THE couch is old and ratty, I can't sit on it. My clothes are soaked in blood, and I'll stain the couch and scare the shit out of the sleeping cat, for sure. *My blood? Ginny's blood? "Ophelia's" grandma's blood? Who knows?* But I don't feel that I can stay on my feet any longer. And next thing I know, I'm sprawled out awkwardly, face down on the floor, seeing stars because I seem to have banged my head on the coffee table when I fainted. My Viking-look-alike hero is kneeling by my side, shaking me gently.

"Hey...hey, let me help you out. We...we can...let's go to the bathroom and get you cleaned up, and I can take a look at your head wound. I don't think it's life-threatening, because if it was...well, if it was, you'd be dead by now." Realizing what he just said, he shrugs his bulky shoulders awkwardly. "Just saying."

I fake a half smile, and he lifts me right off the floor. Although I'm thin, I'm fairly tall, but he doesn't even grimace as he stands up with me in his arms. I don't say a word as he softly places my feet on the floor and leads me to the bathroom.

IT'S CERTAINLY AN unusual feeling to have your bloody clothes carefully removed by a burly, *male* stranger. And once I'm stark naked, to have him stand right beside the shower with his hands on my waist, while I do my best to clean the blood off my body—well, this kind of thing doesn't happen every day. At least not to me. I hang my head and watch as the bloody water swirls around and is swallowed by the drain, and I don't freak out, mainly because I don't think there's any "freak out" left in me. As soon as my head is clean, the guy pulls me out of the shower and forces me to bend at an odd angle so he can examine whatever made my head bleed so much. He studies my scalp for a long time, until I start to shiver and need the spray of hot water to warm me.

When he lets me go, he says, "I think a bullet grazed the top left side of your head. There's a two-inch scrape there, and it's kind of deep. The bleeding's stopped, but you probably ought to get it checked out by a doctor in the morning. It's pretty nasty." His large palm finds its way back to my hip. "But dude, I'd say that, overall, you're pretty lucky, know what I mean?"

Not feeling particularly lucky, I again nod and return to my place beneath the stream of water, wishing I could wash away everything that happened tonight. What's weird is the deep scrape on my head doesn't hurt...nothing does; I'm physically numb. I decide at this moment I'm not going to think about the stuff that hurts my mind until we leave this bathroom...or better yet, until we leave this apartment, which represents a short reprieve between the hell of the shooting and the hell of accepting that it was real.

WE'RE DRY AND sitting on the couch wearing the sweatpants and T-shirts of the guy who lives in this apartment. And I've never been more exhausted in my life. I keep yawning, over and over again. Huge, wide-mouthed intakes of air that leave me feeling intoxicated.

The guy who saved my ass and then acted as my shower monitor turns to me and looks into my eyes in a way I don't think I've ever been looked at before. In his gaze, I see concern and compassion and protectiveness and...and something else I can't pinpoint. Or something I'm too weary to figure out right now.

He says, "I guess maybe it's time we should introduce ourselves. You think?"

I yawn.

"I'm Liam. Liam Norcross."

I stifle another yawn and reply, "Jason Tripp...you can call me Jase."

He reaches for my hand but doesn't shake; he just holds it. As we sit there, hand in hand, my fingers inadvertently tighten on his larger ones. Then his other massive paw joins our hand-holding party, and I once again feel a warm rush of safety, like I did when he'd pressed me beneath the seats in the theater and covered me with his body. "Sorry we had to meet this way, Jase."

Neediness. The emotion I couldn't name that I *still* see in his eyes is neediness. And it seems wrong on this big bear of a man who should be perpetually confident. "Who's Ginny?"

"She is...*was* my girlfriend, ever since freshman orientation week."

"Shit, man. I'm sorry. Shit..."

"She was the first person I met at Batcheldor." I nod and yawn. "I...uh...we were at the theater tonight to see her roommate, Mariah, perform. She was playing Gertrude, Hamlet's mother."

Liam smiles. "I was there to see Mariah too. Mariah Craft, right?"

"Yeah...how do you know her?"

"She's in my marketing class. We're in the same final project group."

Our gazes lock, and although I'm an introverted person by nature, I'm okay with this intense mutual staring. And it hits me that from the time he looked up at me, right before we started holding hands, his eyes have never wavered from mine. "I'm still having trouble believing this is real. I...I..." I'm going to be sick again. I frantically grab an empty popcorn bowl from the coffee table.

I concentrate on the pressure of his hand on my knee, and it turns into a false alarm. "Jase, I know...it was fucked up and awful and..." His deep voice, not so much his words, soothes me. "And *shit*, we've gotta tell somebody about Dom."

"I know we've got to go to the police, but...but, Liam, do you think I can just sleep for a little while first...and then...then I promise..."

"I guess...yeah...just go to sleep, Jase. I'll set the alarm on my phone for a couple of hours, and we'll get up and go to the police then." He finally glances away. "Besides, don't these mass shooter types usually kill themselves when they're done shooting up the room?" He seems hopeful. "Dom's probably already offed himself...so he won't hurt anyone else."

"Yeah, I think they commit suicide before they get caught...usually." I've never been one to watch the news on the days and weeks surrounding school shootings. Too depressing. Too scary. Hits too close to home.

This is a seriously messed-up conversation between relative strangers.

"So a couple of hours shouldn't make a major difference." He sounds unconvinced.

"Liam, thanks...and not just for letting me sleep. Thanks for...everything else you did for me tonight."

His intelligent, brown-eyed gaze softens as it again rests on my face. "Yeah...yeah, no problem."

I just thanked a man for saving my life by saying, "thanks for everything." And he accepted it as if he does heroic shit every day. Maybe he does. I shrug, turn sideways on the couch, and curl up, trying to get comfortable while Liam slides over to the easy chair and kicks up the footrest. But all of the thoughts and memories of what happened in the theater that I've been blocking from my awareness with such determination threaten to return as I settle down and try to sleep. I can feel the memories, like hungry crows, pecking at the protective shell enclosing my consciousness every time I start to drift away. I turn onto my other side but still can't stop those ravenous birds from jabbing and poking, leaving me with no other option but to grab the popcorn bowl. There's nothing in my stomach; all I do is heave.

My guardian angel returns to sit on the far end of the couch, opening his legs and patting the place between them. "Come here." His voice is raspy and infused with emotion so raw it almost hurts to hear as he indicates the place he wants me to be. "Come here, man. Let me help you get to sleep. 'Kay?"

Somewhere in the depths of my throbbing brain, I know that his offer is not "normal" and that two guys aren't supposed to cuddle on a couch, no matter what the circumstance. But I simply nod, shift around, and crawl toward him until my body fills that slot between his legs. His thick thighs close around my hips, and when the sleek black cat snuggles on top of us to share our warmth, it feels like exactly where I'm supposed to be. Which I realize is wrong for thousands of reasons, but I snuggle against him anyway—I place my face on the soft cotton stretched across his broad chest and listen to the miracle of his steady heartbeat, and I luxuriate in the warmth of his arms and legs as they enclose me.

When I wake up, I'll deal with everything. I'll get up off this couch and face the truth...

"THIS IS THE Sanford Police. Open up!"

Don't wanna leave my soft nest...

"We want to talk to you!"

Not ever.

"Open the door now! We know you're in there!"

But my nest starts to move and pull away, and soon I'm a lone baby bird, struggling to stretch my wings in the cold air that now surrounds me.

"Open the door!"

I'm disoriented. I grab the sleeve of my bed partner's sweatshirt as he gets to his feet—it's like some kind of an impulse...as if, by keeping him in this nest, I can prevent the day from dawning.

"Hey, it's gonna be okay, Jase. Looks as if the police just came to us before we got a chance to go to them." His warm hand covers mine.

Despite his comforting gesture, the horror of the night rushes back into my brain. *The theater...the shooter...the earsplitting pops...the smell of blood...Ginny... Oh, God, Ginny!*

"Stay calm, 'kay? I'm gonna go answer the door." Liam's tall blond spikes have slumped to the left side of his forehead, and though he still appears huge and rugged, he seems much younger than before. He picks his glasses up off the coffee table, puts them on, and goes to open the door.

As soon as he swings the door open, six police officers burst inside the apartment, several of them taking Liam to the floor and cuffing his hands behind his back. When two others approach me, Liam loses his cool for the first time since I met him. He bellows, "Leave the kid alone! Don't touch him! Don't you know what he's been through?"

I stand up voluntarily and allow the police to cuff me, if for no other reason than to take that wild look out of Liam's eyes. He needs to think I'm okay with this, even if I'm not.

"We want to ask you a few questions about where you were earlier tonight." A second officer speaks; I can't read his dull tone or his blank expression. "You have the right to remain silent and refuse to answer questions. Do you understand?"

I utter, "I understand," but I don't understand anything at all.

Chapter Three

MAYBE I'M SAFE here, but it's not where I want to be. The only problem with this acknowledgment is that I don't have a clue where I'd rather plant my ass. I have a suspicion that any place I could possibly land right now would be as unappealing as this bland, neutral-colored budget hotel room. It's been thirty-two hours since the shooting—not that I'm counting—and I'm not doing well.

I try to get comfortable on what I've claimed as "my" double bed, but I nonetheless go through the same hell—the kind associated with stuffing down emotions that desperately need to surface—as when I tried to fall asleep alone on Liam's friend's couch on Friday night. Constant nausea, coupled with the inability to block out the persistent thoughts I'm not yet ready to deal with, have me flipping from side to side on the stiff mattress.

Insomnia 101.

Which came first, I ask myself, *the nausea or the restlessness?* Not that it matters. I comfort myself with the knowledge that Mom has been informed I'm okay, so she's most likely worried, but not in the midst of a nervous breakdown.

I'm actually a million miles from "okay," but physically, I'm relatively unharmed.

As it turns out, driving away from the scene of a violent crime makes authorities quite suspicious. Unfortunately, I learned this too late, never having been involved in—or even present at—a violent crime. After intense and extremely intimidating separate interrogations at the police department, it was determined that Liam and I were not accomplices of Domenic William DeSalles, the active shooting suspect in the Batcheldor College Theater Shooting. We're just victims with apparently very bad judgment, considering our decision to cut and run from the scene of a mass murder.

What I've learned since my arrest the night before last, is that Domenic William DeSalles, twenty-one, junior at Batcheldor College majoring in Business Information Systems, has been identified as the alleged solitary gunman in the shooting at the Harrison Theater that killed seventeen and wounded six. And he's still at large, which is the reason I'm being held here in this fifty-shades-of-tan hotel room.

There's a sharp rap on the door, which makes me jump a mile, that's followed by the shouted identification, "Police!" The door swings open, and my heart pounds. Two uniformed officers I don't recognize, the man I've come to know as Detective Spader, and Liam enter the room.

"You've both eaten and are seriously in need of some rest." Spader removes his wire-rimmed glasses and rubs his balding head as if weary, which I'm sure he is, and I silently welcome him to the club. "Go to sleep, and by the time you guys wake up later on today, I'm sure we'll have the suspect in custody, and you'll be able to go back to your normal daily lives. This unfortunate incident will be a thing of the past."

Really? He thinks we can return to Foundations of Physics and keg parties as if this "unfortunate incident" never happened? To go on as if I didn't just witness a bloody slaughter? He's suggesting that I go back to my former life, as if my girlfriend wasn't fatally shot through the brain when we were shoulder to shoulder in a crowded theater? And he expects me to forget that my instinct was to curl up into a fetal ball rather than to attempt CPR, or at a minimum, to hang on to Ginny's hand as she died? *Really, Detective Spader?*

"Thank you, Detective." Liam stops just short of the other double bed and turns to the three law enforcement officers, placing fists on his hips. "I think we can take it from here."

"You know you aren't allowed to leave this room for any reason," Spader reminds us.

Liam and I nod.

"If you need anything, use the cell phone I gave you to call and make a request." He glances from Liam to me, his brow creased, and admits, "We just don't have the manpower to leave a couple guys sitting outside your hotel room to guard you. We've decided the best use of the officers' time is to search for Dom DeSalles. So, yeah, use the phone."

We peer at the cell phone that's on the table between the two beds.

"How's your head, Jason? Do you need to see the doctor again?" Detective Spader asks in afterthought.

I shake my head. I still can't feel any pain.

"Good. Now, there are bottles of water and some snacks in the minibar if you can't wait until we bring you a meal."

The ensuing silence suggests that everything necessary has been said.

"We'll take off then." The three men head for the door. One more time, Spader reminds us, "No leaving this room. And don't open the door for any reason."

The door slams, and Liam and I are alone. It's awkward—neither of us has a clue what to say. Finally, Liam kicks off his boots and falls back on his bed. "How're you holding up?"

I lift the small plastic bag meant to line the ice bucket and wave it in the air. "I'm still hanging on to a barf bag, if that gives you a clue."

Liam's quiet. He probably can't think of a thing to say to a guy who hasn't exactly been the picture of grace under fire. Make that a guy who has crumbled under the pressure like a week-old sugar cookie in a backpack full of textbooks.

"Off to the john," I announce, figuring I can escape from the awkwardness there, and I slide off my bed. When I get to the bathroom, I grip the sides of the sink and glance into the wide mirror to check out the sort of horror show Liam has been looking at for the past day and a half. My close-cropped, dark hair is in place except for the stripe of raw scalp on the top left of my head. My cheeks are gaunt, and I'm pale.

The red rims around my green eyes and dark circles beneath them prevent me from appearing like the "2014 Face of an Angel," which was one of the superlatives I won as a high school senior, among "Most Popular Boy in the Senior Class" and "Boy Most Likely To...wink, wink."

I splash water on my face and brush my teeth one more time. I can't get the taste of death out of my mouth. It takes me ten minutes to feel more mentally together. I leave the bathroom and head back to my bed.

"I know Dom DeSalles from the business program. We both did internships at the Langston Industrial Park last fall," Liam says in a smooth low tone.

I sit on my bed and wait for more. Despite the topic, Liam's deep voice comforts me.

"Plus, we live on the same floor in RetroHouse."

"I live in the RetroHouse basement. I'm one of the few freshmen that got the *privilege* to live in upperclassmen housing." I smirk. "Lucky me." If I lived with the other freshmen, I probably wouldn't have a clue who Dom DeSalles is, and he wouldn't be searching for me so he could blow my brains out since he missed by a few inches on his first attempt.

"I've seen you around. We've passed by each other at the laundry center and in the cafeteria too, I think."

"Gotta have clean clothes and food." I'm not a funny guy, but I deliver the line in what Ginny used to call my *Sponge Bob* voice. It falls flat.

"I've been thinking a lot about Dom." Liam seems to want to talk about the asshole, and I just want to listen to his calm, steady voice, so it's a win-win situation. "He wasn't the friendliest dude on our floor. He always seemed sort of pissed off, like he had a chip on his shoulder, you know?"

"I guess."

"I think his roommate, Mason Maguire, requested a transfer out of their dorm room a couple of weeks ago."

"Really?"

"Yeah. He'd been telling a bunch of us all year that DeSalles was a total head case, and he couldn't put up with it much longer. He didn't say a lot in the way of specifics, but I'll tell you, DeSalles was supposedly bent out of shape when Maguire ditched him."

"Where did Mason end up living?"

"On the RetroHouse third floor in a single that opened up. Cops said that his room got broken into Friday night at dinnertime, but Maguire wasn't there, and a little while later, DeSalles was shooting up the theater."

"So, it was a revenge thing?"

"Could be. Warped, huh?"

"Sure. Makes no sense, really." I turn my back to him. "I'm still wearing your friend's clothes. I don't know if he's gonna want them back any time soon." *Such a stupid thing to say.*

"I don't think he's too worried. Speaking of clothes, I'm gonna pull these off. Can hardly breathe they're so damn tight."

I hear rustling as he pulls off his borrowed clothing, and soon the creak of the bed. Then he seems to settle down.

"You want to tell me about your girlfriend?" Liam's low-pitched voice cracks, and I figure he's nervous. "I'm a pretty decent listener."

"No, not right now." I'm not ready to think, let alone talk, about Ginny. "Sure wish we had a keg."

"Well, when this is all over, I'll take you out for a brew or two."

"I'm not twenty-one. I can't go to a pub."

"Well, I think you earned a couple of beers, surviving that shit the other night. My friend's a bartender at a pub near my house, so you can come visit, and I'll make sure he serves you, 'kay?"

"Sounds like a plan."

The room is dim. The shades are drawn tightly, which makes it seem as if time is standing still. But outside of this room, early morning sun will soon shine onto a new day I'm not ready to face. Before I start to think too much—which seems to lead to major stomach issues, sweating, and a lot of trembling—I shut my eyes and think about baseball, a relatively safe topic.

"Night, Jase," Liam says.

"Good night," I reply, although it's already morning.

I'VE BEEN LYING here for hours, turning from one side to the other, then onto my back and onto my stomach. No matter my position, sleep won't come. I'm shivering then perspiring, and I cling to the plastic bag like it's my security blanket. I use the bathroom and then try to decide if it would be rude to turn on the TV.

I figured he was asleep because his breathing has sounded so even for the past hour, but all of a sudden, Liam pops up out of bed as if he's wide awake too, strides purposefully to the door, and checks that it's bolted. Then he comes to my bed and says in a husky voice, "Move over."

Without a hint of resistance, I slide across the bed so I'm against the wall. Liam stretches out on his back in the middle of the bed, scoops me up, and pulls me onto his bare chest, which is as rugged and furry and manly and safe as the rest of him. I place my head over his heart and listen to the only sound I want to hear—the steady thudding, a reminder that he's very much alive. His arms come around me, and he strokes my back, at first with hesitance, and so softly I can feel the calluses on his palms scratching my shoulder blades. But soon, he kneads my muscles; the tension drains from my back into his fingers. He spends a lot of time working on my neck, as if he can tell it's where most of my anxiety dwells.

"Go to sleep, Jase. Just sleep... We'll figure things out tomorrow." Even though he doesn't specify *how* we'll figure things out, I appreciate the hopefulness in his voice, and I decide that for now, I'm going to believe him. This close to Liam, I'm warm, safe, and comfortable. I close my eyes and drift away.

I WAKE UP crying.

Okay, I'm going to be real: I'm *sobbing*. Sprawled *on top of* the solid chest of a man I hardly know, I sob in a way I never have before. Hopefully, I'll never have occasion to cry this bitterly again.

My emotions are practically indescribable, yet I need to apply words so I can make some sense of what I'm feeling. Mentally, I'm on edge; my pain is raw, grating, and unbearable. I'm guilt-ridden and mortified. Devastation crossed with desperation—this is me, at the moment.

And I'm not sure why I'm still here...on earth. *I want to disappear.*

Liam stays silent, but I know he's awake because his hands have resumed the rhythmic stroking on my back.

"Why'd you have to go and s-save me? Y-you should have let me d-die like I was supposed to!" My fury is evident in the trembling accusation. But my pain would be over if he'd let me die, so I add *mad as hell* to my growing list of emotions.

He inhales deeply. "We're gonna get through this. Our bodies survived Friday night in the theater. Now we've gotta make our minds survive the aftermath."

"What makes you think I *want* to survive it? What makes you so sure I didn't want to go with her?" It's too hard to say her name.

Wide palms freeze on my shoulder blades and rest there heavily. "Sorry, dude, but it wasn't your day to die." He takes another one of those huge gulps of air that causes both of our bodies to rise and fall. Then the mesmerizing movement of his hands picks up where it left off.

Even if it hurts to say her name, I focus on doing justice to Ginny's memory. Although Ginny and I had figured out ours wasn't a forever kind of romance, we also knew that our bond of friendship would last. I admired her for being everything I was not—outspoken, opinionated, and at times, confrontational—and I was one of the few people she trusted implicitly.

"She had dreadlocks." As soon as the words come out of my mouth, I realize this is a strange place to start when describing Ginny's awesomeness. But her long dark dreadlocks were what caught my attention when I saw her standing outside the dining hall on the first day of freshman orientation. "And she hated wearing the nametag they gave her that day...you know, the one that says, '*Hello, my name is so and so.*'" I can't help but smile when I remember how Ginny had unpinned the tag that labeled her *Virginia Eloise Blankenship* as soon as our small group had started on the campus tour. She'd leaned against me and muttered, "Labels are for suckers," and I'd been honored that she'd chosen *me* to enlighten with that shiny pearl of wisdom. "Never saw her in anything but Birkenstocks or bare feet." I smile again. "Kind of dirty-looking bare feet, but they didn't smell bad, or anything like that."

Liam doesn't seem to think the facts I've chosen to share about Ginny are in any way odd. "Were you guys in love?" His voice is husky, possibly sleep-deprived, but more likely indicative of emotional preparation for what he expects me to say.

I, however, reply too quickly for it to be the full story on the subject. "I loved her." I can tell he's nodding because his beard is rubbing up and down against my head, and it hurts. *It hurts...* I can feel the painful throbbing on both the inside and the outside of my head now; something is changing inside me. The tight knot of fear and pain is starting to loosen. "Who were *you* at the play with on Friday night?"

He sighs. I already recognize it as an expression of frustration—of wishing desperately that things could be different. "I couldn't help any of them. It happened too fast...and then I heard a sound from you and so I headed—"

"That's not what I asked." I already know him well enough to understand that he'd have died trying to save his friends. He'd nearly died trying to save me, a perfect stranger.

"There were three of us. It was our marketing final project group. We were creating a sales plan for the product we developed—A Taste of Cinnamon Organic Whitening Strips. I guess the world is going to have to wait for an all-natural, recyclable, and sweetly spicy vehicle for dental bleach."

"Do you think any of them are...you know...still..." I can't make myself say the word *alive*, which is strange.

"No." His response is gruff, and I realize he's in a lot of pain over this. I also realize I'm not crying anymore.

"I...uh...I'm not proud of how I acted...in the theater," I inform him while fighting to suppress what I suspect is going to be a hiccup-sobbing-gaspy thing. But it escapes my lips, anyway, and is louder than I expect. "I...I let go of her hand...after she was shot."

Liam clears his throat and utters, "You never know how you're gonna act when you're scared. You know, *truly terrified*...the way I was on Friday night."

"I always thought I'd be a hero if something like Friday night ever happened and I was around. A hero, like you."

He sniffs, obviously uncomfortable with what I just said. "I'm no hero, Jase. The two guys I went to the theater with died."

"But you...you saved my life."

"Nah." He sniffs again. "I'm no hero. I just pointed you in the right direction."

"You climbed on my back and protected me from getting shot."

"A hero doesn't just lend a hand to the person next to him." He speaks deliberately, as if he's already thought this through. "If I were a *real* hero, I would've attacked that asshole, accepting that maybe I'd have died in the process of saving other people—but that's not what I did, was it? I stayed under the radar while he killed my friends and Ginny and all of those other people...little kids, too! I'm no damned hero."

I disagree with his concept of heroic, but I'm not up for a debate. "I never knew I'd get so freaked out, but I..." I have no good excuse for my failure to act bravely Friday night. And my inaction bothers me but clearly not to the extent his *perceived* inaction messes with Liam's mind.

"There's no way to prepare for fear like that." He speaks as if he's been there before. "You just do what you can to survive."

"I guess so." Even though the discussion is making me uncomfortable, my body is somehow relaxing. The sobbing has taken a lot out of me. But there's something else I need to let him know. "For the record, I'm not... I've never done this kind of thing before...you know, getting this *close* with a guy." My face is burning, and I wonder if he can feel the heat on his chest.

He lifts his head from the pillow at the same time I lift mine from his chest, and we look at each other, which should be extraordinarily awkward, but isn't. The expression in his usually penetrating gaze is soft and gentle and steady—everything that Dom's eyes were not. Not that I saw Dom's eyes on Friday night, but I really didn't need to. I know they were hard and hateful and frenzied. I shudder again.

"Right now we're just two human beings and..." He swallows noticeably and tells me again, "You just do what you can to survive."

I shrug and then lower my head, deciding that analyzing how safe and warm I feel nestled against this rugged man's furry chest can wait until later. And this is when his right hand drags across my hip and squeezes between our bellies. He wraps his long fingers around my dick and holds me, at first hesitantly, and then, when I remain silent, more firmly. I don't move a muscle, not to shove him away or to shout, *"What the fuck do you think you're doing?"*

"I can take your mind off all of this," he says blandly, as if he's offering to read aloud to me from *Harry Potter and the Sorcerer's Stone*. "Let me help."

Neither of us moves, or even breathes, for close to a full minute, during which time my brain scrambles for the right response. On one hand, I want the escape he's offering so badly, and as proof, my dick has swelled enough to fill his palm. But I'm not gay...and I don't know what it *means* to let Liam touch me this way. *Is this just a warped "friends with benefits" thing, or is it one more act of benevolence given by a powerful savior to his needy victim? Does it mean something more?*

And, shit, Liam's the fucking hero in this room. Shouldn't I be the one worshiping *him* with *my* right hand?

My raging thoughts are silenced by the rhythmic movement of his hand. His grip is just right. Nice and tight, but not choking me. And like the rest of him, his hand is huge and rough. My dick fits perfectly in his fist, and the way he's touching me feels like nothing else has...ever.

"Don't stop..." I understand the words, but I don't remember making the decision to speak them. *It doesn't matter.* I drift into the pleasure, justifying it in this way: taking a single short trip away from all the horror won't hurt anyone.

Somehow, Liam knows exactly how I want it. He knows when to move faster, when to grip harder, and at the moment I'm about to come, he grasps my hip with his other hand to let me know I'm not alone—I'm safe with him. He's got my back, and more. I come all over his hand, take an awesome after-the-climax breath...and reality slams me hard.

What the fuck did we just do?

"Um...Liam, I...uh...shit." I have no idea what I want to say to him, but I feel as if I should say *something*. Because, shit, the guy jerked me off, and I let him do it and *liked it*! Before I can come up with a reasonable justification for what went down or even a one-liner to help us laugh it off, I'm sweating, both literally and figuratively. I don't even consider making a polite offer of reciprocation or a weak excuse for the lack of one.

"Think you can go back to sleep now?" It's a simple question, but its frankness efficiently stops the erratic movement of my mind. And for some crazy reason, I find myself relaxing, as if what just happened, never happened.

Instead of answering, I close my eyes and listen to the steady thudding of his heart. It's surprising how quickly I've become addicted to this sound.

I SLEEP SOUNDLY, far better than I would have expected. Because of this, when I wake up, the guilt is overwhelming. *How could I sleep like a baby when I so recently witnessed the slaughter of seventeen innocent men, women, and children—including my very own girlfriend?*

And I'd love to say I've forgotten about what Liam and I did last night, but it isn't something I can sweep under the rug, which leads to more guilt and an entirely unique sense of panic. Naturally, I refuse to accept the minor detail that I'm aroused *right now*, as I lie on the massive chest of this man I hardly know, but who knows my mind, and now my body, better than anyone else.

I should recoil from Liam's chest as if he's a burning bush I've fallen upon, but I can't. My fingers actually tighten on his biceps.

"You're awake." I wait for him to push me off him, which is what I'd expect a straight guy to do, but he doesn't move a muscle. None of this makes sense.

"I...I'm..." And just like last night, I can't think of a thing to say. Nothing at all. Thankfully, the phone rings, saving me from blurting out, "Oh my freaking God, I let you jerk me off last night!"

Liam hesitantly unwraps his arm from my shoulder and stretches to pick up the phone from the night table. As it seems to be the correct thing to do, I force myself to sit up and hop off the bed, then cross the two-foot space of cream-colored rug where I drop down on the bed Liam had once claimed as his. He listens to the person on the other end of the line, swallows hard, and says, "You're kidding me."

I don't like the sound of this at all. Whatever it was that just loosened inside me enough to let me sleep like the dead, tightens.

"Has anybody seen him?"

All too quickly, I'm getting the picture.

"So we're supposed to just stay here...until...until..."

I stand and head to the minibar hoping there's something sweet enough to give me the energy I'm going to need to deal with what Liam's about to tell me. On top of the minifridge is a basket of candy bars, and I randomly pull one out and take a bite and then another, during which time Liam ends the call. By the time I take a third bite, he's set the phone on the night table.

He sighs that way I already know so well.

"What's the word?"

He sits and swings his legs over the edge of the bed. "Looks as if you and me are gonna be hanging here for a while longer."

I turn around and glare at him. "Tell me why."

"They can't find him, Jase. Dom DeSalles is missing." He stands, and his massiveness again catches me by surprise, but I manage to swallow back my gasp. And although I'm newly astounded at his potential for physical power... I'm glad of it. Maybe he's the only one who can keep me safe.

Chapter Four

THE GOOD NEWS is that the police take care of all the details. We're provided with meals, comfortable clothing from a local sports shop, and—since we're technically off the grid—they've explained the situation to our families. I'm most grateful they informed Mom about my precarious situation, lifting that burden from my shoulders. I don't envy them the task; she's high-strung, and my safety has always been her top priority. She's rather obsessed by it.

Meanwhile, Liam and I are stuck in a time warp where we can't extend condolences to the relatives of those who were killed or share memories of the horrifying event with other survivors. As the police search doggedly for Dom DeSalles, the two of us remain hidden. And with only each other to turn to, that's exactly what we do.

"How well did you know Dom DeSalles?" I ask. We're stretched out on our backs with our hands behind our heads, on individual double beds, more or less watching television. At some point last night, we found a station that shows baseball games—live and pre-recorded—pretty much 24/7. Baseball is just the game we need to help us pass the time. Not too angst-filled, unless there's a bench-clearing brawl, which is rare. It makes decent background noise if you want to talk or sleep, but can also engage your brain, when necessary.

"Not very well. We're both in the business program, so we've had a few classes together. And we did the internship last summer." He turns onto his side to face me. "I invited him to sit with me in the cafeteria at lunchtime—every day of the first week of the internship—but he refused to look at me, let alone reply. So I gave up and just hung out with other guys from my department."

"Who did he eat lunch with?"

"He sat alone, but the weird thing is, he seemed pissed off at me...as if *I'd* rejected *him* or something." Liam is huge...imposing, even when lying on a bed. I can't imagine ignoring him right to his face. "And the guy doodled a lot."

"Doodled?"

"Yeah...he was always drawing in this spiral-bound notebook. He kept it pretty close to his vest, but whenever I walked by and glanced down, I saw pictures of weapons—rifles and crossbows and stuff like that—and people lying around bleeding. I figured he had a vivid imagination and pushed it out of my mind."

I close my eyes to absorb his words, and I hear that familiar sigh.

"I should've done something. But I just shook my head and walked away and...my failure to act got a whole lot of innocent people killed."

"You couldn't have stopped what happened, Liam. He probably had it all planned out right down to the very last bullet."

He flips onto his side and faces the wall. "I'm gonna try and catch a few Z's, man."

"Okay, that's cool. Maybe I'll do the same." I don't make a move to roll onto my side; I just close my eyes and wait for sleep to come.

And wait.

And wait.

Sadly, I'm getting used to sleep's refusal to show up when I need it most. But part of me is thankful for it. Ever since I was a kid, when something weighs on my mind, I have nightmares. Even if I watch a horror movie, or eat too much ice cream too close to bedtime, my dreams reflect it. So it's probably just as well I can't fall asleep.

"DON'T SHOOT HER! Leave us alone!" My own screaming wakes me up. "Don't! Please...no!"

In a split second, I'm scooped into strong arms. Still bracing myself—ready for the explosion and the pain and the anguish—I hear a voice. "It's over, Jase...you're safe. You're safe now."

More than I want my next breath, I want to stay safe and warm in this fortress that shelters me, but I can't. I struggle to free myself from the protective, addictive arms. "But Ginny! *My Ginny*—she's dead! He shot her and...and her head fell to the side... I could feel it drop onto my shoulder... And there was warm wet stuff on my face... It was Ginny's *blood* splashing out... I think it was coming out of her ear, but maybe it was coming out of her temple where the bullet...where it went in and..." Although my eyes are wide open and I'm staring at a beige ceiling, I don't have a clue where I am. And I'm shivering like I'm five years old and I just climbed out of the bathtub and ran—wet and naked—down the hallway to my bedroom to find my PJ's, while Mom yells, "You're gonna catch a cold, Jason— mark my words—you're gonna catch your death!"

"You couldn't have helped her, Jase. There was nothing you could do." Liam's voice is familiar, his arms are sturdy, and his presence is steady— He's all I want, and just what I need. "She died instantly."

His words are difficult to hear, although I recognize their truth. I'm so lost. "Where are w-we?"

"In the safe house...the hotel the police put us in to keep Dom from finding us."

I nuzzle into his chest. Like a baby connecting with its mother, I breathe in his scent. And then I roll around until I'm nestled perfectly in his arms. "Why do I need you so much? Why am I addicted to your arms and your voice and your sound and your smell?"

"I don't know."

"You saved me." He smells like sweet mint and almonds, the best parts of nature...and I can't get enough. I push my nose into the hollow of his neck and brace myself for rejection, but it doesn't come. Neither does he offer to repeat our sexual interaction of the other night. I *think* I'm relieved, but maybe it's just disguised disappointment.

"You saved me right back. Saving you saved me." Strong fingers tighten on my hip and shoulder, and I know instinctively that everything in my life has changed.

Chapter Five

I'M *SO* NOT myself that I don't even recognize the sound of the cell phone. Its shrill ring brings me back to the night in the theater when the fire alarm screamed. Startled, I peer around the bland room for a fire...or a crazed gunman. The blood races through my veins as adrenaline surges.

"It's okay, Jase. It's just the phone." His palm easily finds my knee where it lingers, and I stare at it, wondering why my heart slows back to its normal pace with this man's mere touch. "It's gotta be the police. No one else has this number. I can call them back when you feel better."

We're sitting cross-legged on the bed we've recently adopted as *ours*, halfheartedly playing gin rummy. Liam more or less set up camp on my bed after my major freak-out last night, and I'm grateful. "No...it's okay. Go ahead and answer. It might be important."

Once again, he leans and grabs the cell phone off the night table. "Yes? Yeah...this is Liam. *She did what?* Jesus Christ, gimme a goddamn break!"

Liam is a different man than thirty seconds ago. His skin has paled, his expression is suddenly stressed; his hand tightens painfully on my knee.

"Where the fuck are we supposed to go, Spader?" He isn't smiling. "The fucking *laundry room*? You got any better ideas than that?"

The fight or flight response.

I learned about it in Intro to Psychology, an elective I took senior year in high school. It's defined as an instinctive response to a perceived danger that tells you to get the hell out of Dodge if you don't plan to fight for your very survival with everything you've got. My heart pounds so intensely that I can feel it in my eardrums, and the skin under my arms prickles. I leap off the bed, ready to run, because judging by the expression on Liam's face, something has gone wrong in the plans to keep us safe.

"Okay, okay...we're leaving." Liam drops the cards he was holding and gets off the bed but doesn't reach for me. "Yeah, we're going *right now*. We'll meet you in the housekeeping suite." He ends the call and stares at me in a state of controlled panic.

"What's the matter, Liam? What's going on?" My voice is shrill—I don't even try to play it cool. The composed appearance I've managed to fake for the past few hours washes away like blood down a bathtub drain.

"We've gotta get outta here, ASAP! Jase, they think Dom knows..."

"Dom knows *what*?"

"He knows where we are."

"H-how? H-how does he know? We're supposed to be safe here!" I put my head in my hands and mumble *what the fuck, what the fuck*, over and over until I can breathe again.

"Some friggin' idiotic news station televised a broadcast from right in front of this hotel. The reporter talked about how two witnesses are being held at an undisclosed location, but *this hotel* was visible in the background. It wouldn't take a genius to figure it out, and Dom's damned sharp. We can't risk it by just sitting on our asses and waiting for him to show up and..."

"No...n-no..." I'm terrified; even my knees are wobbling. "This can't be happening...*what the fuck...what the fuck...*"

"Look, Jase. We've gotta head out—as in, *now*!" He grabs my sneakers from beside the bed and shoves them into my hands. "Put these on. Detective Spader and a whole slew of cops are already on their way, and they told me we should meet them in the housekeeping unit in the basement...in the room with all of the washers and dry—"

His explanation is interrupted by three loud thuds on the door.

Three ominous terrifying thuds that bring back memories I haven't yet fully grasped, let alone come close to dealing with.

And I know as well as Liam that not a single soul, with the exception of the police, has a clue we're here. Detective Spader even told housekeeping that the boys in 312 didn't need cleaning service. And didn't he say the police would always identify themselves when they knocked?

Our gazes collide; we know who has come to call.

Liam's brain seems to be on the same path as mine, but I slide into my typical immobilized panic mode—gawking at the door with a sneaker in each hand—where he springs into action. "We're gonna have to use the window."

Pop-pop-pop...

Is that the sound of actual *gunfire, or is this another nightmare?*

I *think* I cry out, "Not again!" But who can be sure in times like these?

Then I hear it: a strangely cheerful, singsong bass voice calling to us from behind the door. "I told you I'd find you...and unlike *some* people, I keep my promises." I have no idea what he means by that, but he seems to find it funny.

He laughs, and the sound is creepy. "Just like my old man always says, a person is only as good as his word."

I fumble with my sneakers.

"Jason—forget the damned sneakers! Get your ass over here *now*!" Liam's standing by the window, pushing out the screen. *"Now!"*

I shake my head hard, hoping it will rouse me from this bad dream, and I somehow obey. Still barefoot, I drop my sneakers and move to the window.

Pop-pop-pop...

The door splinters in several places. I can see through to movement on the other side, which seems terrifying and unreal. Moisture dribbles down the side of my chin as I've lost my ability to swallow.

Liam grabs me roughly and shoves me through the open window, just as he pushed me through the trapdoor to the orchestra pit several nights ago. I can feel his heat behind me on the landing of the narrow fire escape. My forearm is gripped tightly, and I think of fingerprint bruises. And of how lucky I'll be if I live to see the evidence of Liam's second show of heroism in small dark bruises up my arm.

Déjà vu and then some, huh?

Pop-pop-pop...

One bullet hits the inside window frame, another flies right through the open window and whizzes past my head. *If I just stand still, I can join Ginny...wherever she is.* I cheated death once, but apparently, the Grim Reaper has my number.

"I'm not leaving you here, Tripp! I didn't leave you *then*, and I'm not gonna leave you *now*!" Liam's dark eyes are wide with fear and something else...something like resolve. I allow my trembling limbs to be dragged in his wake, to the creaky stairs, and then down.

The shooter—Dom DeSalles, minus all the threatening black clothing of Friday night—leans out the window that we climbed from fifteen seconds ago. Minds are funny things, and right now, mine is thinking that this version of Dom, in a bright red Nike "Just Do It" T-shirt and messed up dark curls, seems sort of boyish, as if he just rolled out of bed. But instead of a teddy bear, he's clutching a handgun... Aside from in sports shops and outdoor magazines, I've never before seen one close up. And never before in the light of day have I seen a gun pointed directly at my head at the distance of ten feet.

The sight of my intended assassin holds me spellbound. And Dom is equally transfixed by me, but in an entirely different way. His eyes are unnaturally round; the whites seem to diminish the size of his eyeballs. And he's smiling—a satisfied "I told you so" leer.

Even if it's not the rifle of my nightmares, the sight of a black-and-silver handgun directed at my face sends chills of dread racing up my spine. Instead of running, I brace myself, unwilling to get shot without being ready for it. But before I hear the deafening crack of the first of three shots, surely to be accompanied by the blinding pain of having my forehead ripped apart by scorching metal, I'm tackled and slammed to the ground. For a second, Liam is on top of me, but he scrambles to his feet, picks me up, shoves me in front of him, and shelters me by curving himself around my body. A mutual stumble and fall to the bottom of the rusty stairs puts us momentarily out of Dom's line of fire. Surprisingly, probably to all three of us, Liam and I have made it to the hotel parking lot relatively intact.

Without thinking, I scan the nearly empty lot for a cherry-red muscle car, but I don't see it, and then I remember that we were delivered to this "safe house" in unmarked cop cars.

Pop-pop-pop... Pop-pop-pop...

"Get behind that truck, Jase!" Liam again drags me to my feet and pushes me in the direction of a white Ford Tundra. Apparently still coherent, my brain sends the order to my legs, and I manage to step behind the vehicle. But my heart isn't invested in this second escape from the crazed gunman who is determined to kill us for no reason I can come up with. I curl into a tight ball, reminiscent of the fetal position I formed on the theater floor before Liam found me. I'm so far less than the measure of a man—I'm weak and scared and...and surprisingly less disappointed in myself than I'd ever have predicted.

Pop-pop-pop...

Liam hasn't curled up on the pavement beside me, though. He's standing behind the truck, shifting around and seemingly trying to keep an eye on the madman. "Shit! DeSalle's climbing out the window!" Liam shakes me until I release myself from the fetal position. "Get ready to run!"

I'm supposed to run through this parking lot, dodging bullets that have my name written on them? Really?

"And when you run, you gotta kinda zigzag..." He gestures awkwardly, trying to explain. "Don't run in a straight line. He's not a great shot, so chances are good he'll miss us!"

Chances are... His choice of words makes me want to smile; they strike me as whimsical and romantic, which this situation certainly is not. My mind isn't into the fight or flight thing—it's way too much to deal with. I'm strangely apathetic when I wonder about our odds of surviving this sunny Tuesday morning in the parking lot of the Sleep and Stay Hotel.

The Sleep and Get Shot At Hotel. I suppress a giggle and coil into a snakelike spiral.

"He's climbing down the stairs... We've gotta run!" Liam tugs on my forearm to get my attention. "Jason! Man, you're coming with me... You hear me—you're coming with me!" He pushes on my shoulder and scratches the side of my legs to uncoil me, but I'm too caught up in the hollow sound of the shooter's footsteps as they approach, to move.

"L-leave me here...just g-go...go..." Beneath the truck, I now see a pair of black-and-white Nike LeBron Soldiers, an interesting choice of shoes to wear to a murder.

Something is seriously wrong with my brain; I'm more interested in Dom's sneakers than his close proximity. "Liam... just leave me here..." My head has closed up shop because I can't cope with this much fear. But Liam shouldn't have to die here with me. "Go on...get out of here, Liam...I'm cool with it."

"I'm not leaving you," Liam replies softly, all of his panic, suddenly gone. With a shake of his head, Liam drops to his knees and covers me with his bulk.

Pop-pop-pop...

Next thing I know, the parking lot fills with police cars, sirens blaring. A huge van pulls up beside us, and a rush of SWAT guys try to pull Liam off me, but he won't let go.

There's a clamor of shouting—orders and threats directed at Dom and Liam—and a single gunshot coming from the shooter's direction.

Pop!

"Liam!" I scream as I'm dragged away behind a hulking policeman and his protective shield. In making my graceless exit from the chaotic scene, I can't stop screaming.

Part Two

July

Chapter Six

"ALL I'M SAYING is that you aren't the same— never have been—since *that thing* happened in April."

"That thing" is how Mom refers to the theater shooting.

"And if you'd just listen to me for once in your twenty years, you'll transfer out of that hillbilly college up in the sticks of Vermont and enroll in the far superior college in your very own hometown." She's standing over my usual spot on the couch, shaking a wooden spoon at me, as this debate erupted halfway through her making the double-chocolate fudge brownie recipe she's so proud of. "You can live at home, and I can keep your laundry clean and cook for you, too."

"Mom...I'm okay. I'll be fine when I get back to Batcheldor."

"Fine like you were *the first* or *the second* time that whacko tried to shoot you dead?"

I'm used to her saying this kind of stuff, but it still sends shivers up my spine.

"You quit your job at the Quik-Mart last month—admit it Jason—it was because you were afraid somebody would pull a gun on you, which honestly concerned me, too. And you just sit here on the couch day after day—no job, no girlfriend... You aren't even seeing Kendrick and Dan, and they're your best friends."

Were my best friends...before I met Ginny.

Next, she's going to dismiss my therapy as "expensive and totally ineffective." I know the woman well.

"And that psychobabble doctor you've got...Dr. Jeffries...well, don't get me started on him." A blob of brownie batter flies off the spoon she's waving and lands on my knee. I just leave it there because who really cares? "If seeing that headshrinker was doing you any good, honey, you'd be all better by now." Her tone suddenly turns from nagging to sweet. "Stay here in Wilson, Jase, and let Mama take care of you." She leans down to caress the side of my face, but I turn away.

"Mom..." She doesn't understand PTSD, which is what Dr. Jeffries says I have, but then I don't fully get it either. Still, I try to control the sharpness in my voice. This isn't my mother's fault. "I'm getting better. Just give me some time." I rise from the couch and go to my bedroom where I spend ninety percent of my life. *If I make it one hundred percent, I won't have to deal with Mom anymore.* Solitary confinement actually sounds tempting.

My room has turned into an escape from the past and present, and it's starting to look like I'll be spending my future here too. It's the only place I feel safe—from crazed gunmen and Mom's draining lectures. I was at a college performance of *Hamlet*, and I was nearly killed; I'm no dummy, and I realize the risk of working at a convenience store. They're robbed at gunpoint all the time. It makes sense that certain enclosed places—like stores and trains and, of course, theaters—are just too hard for me to deal with. I can't go through that level of pain again; nothing is worth the risk.

For a while, I thought my symptoms were part of a normal response to a traumatic event. There are nightmares and obsessive thoughts—I replay the two near-death experiences in my head, over and over again. And there is the emotional numbness I experience—my goals have slipped away, as have my relationships. All normal, Dr. Jeffries says. But the "normal response" refuses to go away—or even diminish—over the passage of time. Something is wrong with me. Messed-up-in-the-head-big-time wrong.

I left school right after the second attack. Thankfully, Batcheldor College allowed a pass on final exams to any student who was having severe emotional difficulties with regard to the theater shooting. As soon as I checked out of the hospital and was declared "fine," I went home to the loving arms of my overprotective single mother. My roommate, BJ, packed up my stuff in the dorm room because I just couldn't bring myself to do it. I retreated to Wilson, New Hampshire, and the safety of home.

I never even reached out to say goodbye to Liam, who'd twice saved my life and my sanity. I'm not sure why I left without saying goodbye. It's just what I did. And I'm almost certain I did it for the same reason that I never allow myself to think about him. *Never*. Too much pain associated with his memory. And then there's the confusion.

Once in my room, I stop in front of the full-length mirror and glance at my reflection. My jeans are barely hanging on to the curve of my ass, and my T-shirt is bagging off me. Technically, I've been starving myself. It's not really intentional— I'm just never hungry anymore.

I'm starting to realize that running away has not been successful in helping me bypass emotional distress. I've avoided certain physical reminders—the school buildings and the college town, people like Liam who bring back the memories so vividly—but my flashbacks are as real as the shootings, themselves. Just like the night of the theater shooting, time is again standing still. Weeks have passed me by, and it still feels as if the shootings happened yesterday. And as if another shooting could happen at any moment. I guess pain that hasn't been dealt with follows you wherever you go.

I throw myself down on my freshly made-by-Mom bed and try not to think, but the more I try to keep my head blank, the more intrusive the thoughts of the attacks become.

Something's got to give. I can't go on this way.

My cell phone rings. It's a sound I've come to dread, as on the other end is always someone I have no interest in being interrogated by, like my high school pals who just *don't get* the new Jason who doesn't ever want to leave his house. I don't recognize the number, which means it could be a random reporter doing a news story on mass shootings. I need to relive that experience like I need another hole in my head. *Ugh, so not funny.* But on the off chance it's the girl who'd been in a terrible car accident that I gave my number to—from the PTSD support group at the clinic Dr. Jeffries encouraged me to join—I have a responsibility to answer.

"Hello."

"Jase?"

I'm pretty sure I know the voice. And for a split second, I experience a sensation of relief, similar to the one I had when I learned that the final gunshot—on the day Dom tracked us down at the hotel to kill us—had been Dom taking his own life and not ending Liam's. "This is Jase."

I have no doubt who's on the phone when he allows his trademark sigh. "I'm, uh...just calling to...to..."

"To check in on me?"

"Well, yeah. I guess...something like that."

"I'm still alive and kicking. And no crazed gunman has taken me out since we last saw each other." I hope he can hear the smile in my voice, even if it's fake.

"Well, that's a step in the right direction." I'm pretty sure he doesn't buy my happy-go-lucky tone.

"I want to see you, Jase. And I'm going to Massachusetts on Friday, for a weekend on Cape Cod. I want you to come with me."

Liam Norcross is the most direct reminder of the worst two nights of my life. "I...I've got to work." It's not easy to lie to him.

Silence.

"And I don't think my mom is ready for me to go anywhere yet."

"'Kay."

"Plus, I...I don't think I'd be too much fun to hang out with. I'm not exactly a barrel of laughs these days."

"Why don't you let me be the judge of that?"

I want to see him. I need to. I wish he'd plead with me, or insist that I go with him. Order me to do it, the way he did when he forced me to stay safe on the nights we were in so much danger.

"I *need* to see you, Jase. This...this visit is really more about me than you." Again, he sighs, and it sounds more pained than I remember. "Will you come with me? Please."

"When will you pick me up?" All I can see in my mind's eye are Liam's arms. So strong and protective and everything I needed...everything I need. For months, all I could see when I closed my eyes was Dom. And now I see Liam.

Chapter Seven

MOM IS ABOUT to lose it.

When I first told her my plans to go to the Cape for the weekend, her response was to laugh in my face. "I'll believe it when I see it, Jason. You haven't moved from that couch in days except to go pee or hide in your bed."

As she watched me pack my bag on Friday afternoon, her tune changed slightly. "So tell me about this man who is supposedly 'rescuing you' from your mother and the safety of your home this weekend."

"His name is Liam Norcross, Mom. He's the guy who saved my life." *Twice.*

Mom's mouth had fallen open, apparently unable to come up with a challenge.

She became more direct when I sat in the chair by the window to watch for Liam to pull up in his Charger. "What makes you think that just the sight of this young man isn't going to send you right back to where you were in April? Always shaking and sweating and hiding in your room. Tell me that, young man."

I had no smart comeback, other than to point out that I still spend significant time shaking, sweating, and hiding.

When his car pulls into the driveway, Mom asks me, "Are you sure it's a good idea to miss your Sunday afternoon support group meeting?" She's always tried to tell me that the PTSD support group is a colossal waste of my time, so I know she's grasping at straws. Mom's as scared to let me out of her sight as she is to let someone else take charge of my safety.

"Mom, I love you, and I'll call you when I get to Cape Cod. Try to have a nice weekend." Before I step out the front door, she grabs me and squeezes, clinging to my shoulders, and I know she loves me, too, but she doesn't know how to do it in the way I need right now.

LIAM TURNS SIDEWAYS to study me when I climb into the car. He's quiet, taking me in boldly, his eyes roving from my head to my toes and back. Finally, he says, "Your hair grew back where the bullet...you know."

I nod, aware that I'm studying him with equal attention to detail. And then I make my big confession. "I left school and never said goodbye to you."

"Yeah, I know." I'm struck by how good he looks. His blond hair is standing tall and his light beard shaped into a long rectangle. And I think he's been working out because his shoulders are bulkier than I remember, and his biceps are bigger beneath his black Coldplay T-shirt. I'm surprised it isn't the memory of fear and pain that return to me, but instead, the strength and the warmth he offered when he held me.

"I'm sorry about that, Liam. I appreciate what you did for me. I wouldn't be here if not for you."

"The feeling is mutual." I peer at him with a question in my eyes, because I did *nothing* to save him. He adds, "I'll explain that later this weekend."

Still parked in my driveway, we sit in silence. I lean back in my seat, blow out the breath in my chest, and take in the secure feeling I hadn't realized I missed. "I'm glad you called."

Liam shrugs. "I guess it's time to get this show on the road." He backs out of the driveway, and I fight the urge to reach out and touch his strong shoulder.

This is the first time since April that the idea of going forward in life seems tolerable. It's as if seeing him—having him beside me—gives me hope. My response to Liam *is* quite unique, and I don't think it's just because of that one night we messed around. But now isn't the time to question myself. My plan is to follow along behind Liam, like I did back in April when chaos reigned. Maybe he can save my life for the third time.

AFTER SEVERAL HOURS of driving with the bare minimum of conversation, we arrive at a little cottage near the Bourne Bridge. It's just after nine o'clock at night. The place is nothing spectacular—a modest 1970s beachfront cottage with what I imagine are spectacular views of the bay in daylight. The exterior is rustic—some may say it had seen better days—but the sense of escape in this little house is palpable. The interior is just what I expected based on the outside: couches draped in floral sheets that look as if they belong to somebody's grandmother, tables covered in plastic tablecloths, and *Your Visit to Cape Cod* magazines stacked up in old-fashioned wooden racks.

"I have a buddy at work whose parents own this place. They rent it out for most of the summer, but there was a last-minute cancellation for this weekend, so they offered it to me." Liam places the pizza we picked up on the plastic-lined kitchen table, and I place the case of beer beside it. "They're great people. Wouldn't let me pay a cent."

"That was nice of them." I glance around at the unfamiliar environment and wait to experience the anxiety

I've grown accustomed to...and that has plagued me since the shootings. Despite a slight chill of wariness, I'm fine. "Where's your summer job, Liam?"

"I work in a pub on the ocean in Lockwood, my hometown in Maine. Mostly I do the heavy lifting, janitorial work, and upkeep of the building. Not too glamorous but I like it."

I picture burly Liam lugging beer kegs and cleaning the floors using a 26-quart janitor's rolling bucket with a mop sticking out of the mop wringer. "So you don't cook?"

"Nah, they don't trust me too much in the kitchen. My buddy, Tommy, is the main fry cook, and his Dad tends the bar. He's got a couple of younger sisters who do the serving and bussing, and his mom does the books."

"They keep it *almost* all-in-the-family."

"Yeah, except for me. I've worked there since I turned sixteen. The Deweys take care of me."

The fact that he doesn't mention his own family hits me as strange, but I don't ask about it. I wonder how the Deweys feel about Liam's multiple brushes with death this past spring. But I offer him some truth instead of asking questions. "I stopped working about a month ago. Just couldn't cope with being behind the counter in a convenience store, you know?"

Liam drops his duffel bag on the floor and relieves me of my backpack, putting it carefully on the floor beside his bag. "Yeah, I feel ya." I think he actually gets it, too. "Sit down and I'll serve you." The little cottage has an open floor plan; he gestures toward the couch in the living room area.

"A guy could get used to this treatment." I walk to the couch and sit, all the while watching as Liam searches the cupboard for plates and then stacks them and some beers on top of the pizza box.

"Well, go ahead and get used to it...for the weekend, at least. You're my guest, and I'm gonna treat you right." Our gazes meet, and I feel a zing of human connection I haven't experienced since I last saw him. He winks and breaks the spell. We dive into the pizza.

"I haven't been this hungry in a long time...it's good." I'm suddenly ravenous and shove the pizza in my mouth with a gusto I thought I'd lost forever.

"You look as if you dropped a few pounds, man. So go on and chow down."

He probably wants to ask me why I've been starving myself but holds back.

Maybe he hopes I'll voluntarily explain my near-skeletal state. Too bad I have no decent explanation other than that I haven't been very hungry lately.

We eat in silence, and when the pizza is gone, I get up to take the plates to the sink.

"Sit down and drink your beer. I'll go get us a couple more."

When he leaves, the lighthearted atmosphere leaves with him. He returns with the beers and his expression is serious. The time to talk has come. I want desperately to know how he's doing in the aftermath of the shootings, and if he feels as alone and scared and numb as I do, but I can't bring myself to ask. So I lift my beer to my lips and wait.

"I've thought a lot about you, Jase." He sniffs and then rubs his nose. "I can't stop thinking about you, to be honest."

"What do you mean?"

He runs his huge hands through his blond hair. "I don't quite understand...you know, what's going on in my head. But I figure I've got to be thinking about you so much because I need to know how you're doing. I must need to know you're okay, or something. Right?"

I nod. What he said makes sense, although it isn't how I handled *my* stress. I'd simply blocked him out of my mind along with every other reminder of the theater shootings. "If you want to know how I am, honestly, I've seen better days."

"I had a feeling…"

"It's hard for me to live at home. It's as if I'm stuck in a rut. Mom doesn't want me to go back to Batcheldor at all because of what happened. Part of me agrees with her and thinks I should stay at home and attend the university in my town where I'll be safe. But another part of me knows that if I don't go back to Batcheldor College, I'll never move on."

"Well…" Liam plays with his long beard, clearly deep in thought. "Let's see if we can't get you out of that rut this weekend. 'Kay?"

His words are upbeat, but he's not smiling. And I'm confused. A lot about Liam confuses me. "Why are you doing all this for me?"

"We'll talk about that later this weekend, I promise. But right now, how about if we just try to find some comedy on TV, suck down a couple brews, and kick back?"

Despite being curious about Liam's reasons for looking out for me so attentively, I'm relieved to experience this reprieve from my own emotional torment. Something about Liam's presence has me breathing easier. "Sounds like a plan to me."

We end up drinking all night. Most people would think that plenty of talking would accompany all that drinking, but we quietly watch stand-up comedy and then an old black-and-white war movie, and then we find an '80s Big Hair Band Countdown to the Top Rock Ballad, which pretty much gets us to sunrise.

"Wanna go to the bedrooms and crash?" Liam asks when the sun starts to peek in the window. "I'll take one of the bunk beds, and you can have the room with the double bed."

"Why can't we just stay here and sleep?" I'm drunk, but not too drunk to know that tomorrow I can blame my suggestion that we sleep together on having overindulged. My typical cop-out.

We're still fully dressed, shoes and all, sitting on either end of this lumpy floral beast of a sofa that's probably older than both of us put together. Upon my suggestion, he slides down on its outside edge and pats the spot between him and the back of the couch. "Join me, won't you?"

I scramble beside him and wedge my newly skinny body between him and the couch. He sighs, and I remember the sound. It makes me smile. "You always sigh..."

"Sometimes I sigh when I want something I just can't have." I'm not too drunk to wonder about his remark.

I face the high back of the couch, and I wish so much I could turn around and push my face against the softness of Liam's T-shirt. But in doing that, I'd be going to a place where I wasn't invited. It would be almost like asking for a kiss, and since neither of us is gay, that would be wrong. So I cross my arms in front of my chest and enjoy the feeling of being spooned by someone I feel safe with. And I find it difficult to talk myself out of being aroused, giving me another reason to be thankful that I'm not pushed up against him, face-to-face. My not so little secret would surely be revealed. Of course, I blame my stiff dick on my drunken state.

I lie here with him, feeling his steady heartbeat against my back, and thriving in the intimacy. Being close to Liam also brings me back to memories of being close to Ginny. She too always wanted to spoon me from behind. I smile, thinking I must be very "spoonable." Since the shooting, this is the first time I've thought about Ginny without feeling sick.

Liam's furry chin drops onto my shoulder, returning me to the here and now, and his dependable arms work their way around my shoulders. I don't think I could ask for anything more.

But as my eyes start to blink and close, I let myself wonder what it is he wants enough to sigh about.

Chapter Eight

DESPITE A NASTY hangover, this is the best Saturday I've had in months.

"Aaaahhhh! I'm never gonna live this down—I forgot all about calling my mother last night. She probably thinks you're Ted Bundy and you took me to your evil dungeon to roast me and eat my flesh and make a scarf out of my skin."

"You're mixing up your serial killers. I'm pretty sure they'd be offended if they knew." Liam smiles, and I notice that his teeth are not only chalk white but are also perfectly straight, and I'm surprised. I have a hard time picturing him as a twelve-year-old boy with awkward silver braces decorated with red, white, and blue elastics, or as an adult wearing whitening strips. This last thought reminds me of the organic cinnamon-flavored whitening strips his marketing group was working on before the shooting, and I fight the urge to dig a hole in the sand and stick my head into it. Memories of the shooting still have this kind of effect on me.

"What's the matter, Jase?" We're lying on matching pink bath towels on the white sandy beach behind our cottage, heads and feet in the sand. We spent the morning alternately swimming and eating dry toast, thanks to the ocean in our front yard and a loaf of bread left in the freezer by the cottage's former guests. "What just crossed your mind?"

"You don't want to know, Liam… I think I should reply to Mom's twenty-seven texts."

He lets me off the hook and laughs. "You don't want to hold off until she reaches the round number of thirty? I don't think you'll have to wait very long at this rate."

I shake my head. "Knowing my mother, she's had a tracking device implanted in my cell phone. She'll show up here if I don't let her know I'm okay."

"It's cool that she loves you so much." His smile falls.

I wonder about the change in him but shrug and send off the "I'm okay, Ma, so don't panic" text.

"I thought I'd treat you to a burger tonight. Tommy said there's a great little pub just up the street; we might catch the Red Sox game. They're playing Toronto, I think."

We watched a lot of baseball in the (un)safe house.

"It'll be fun. We can go for the happy hour dinner special. Man cannot live on bread—or in our case, toast—alone." He gets up and offers me his hand. I take it, and we run into the cottage to rinse off the sand.

THE BEACHCOMBER BAR and Grille is a lively pub that serves fine seafood and is also a pickup joint. At least it is at happy hour. Liam's friend Tommy forgot to mention this minor detail. Based on the steady hum of hormones flying through the air, I have a sneaking suspicion Liam is going to learn the lesson of not asking Tommy the right questions about local eating establishments the hard way. And because I'm barely twenty and I don't have a fake ID, Liam has decided to toss back virgin lemonades right along beside me. In any case, our heads are clear, which turns out to be a good thing.

"Go ahead and have a beer. I don't mind." There's no need for both of us to stay sober. "You can get toasted, and I can drive the Charger back to the cottage."

"I had too much 'toast' this morning." Liam smiles and his teeth look even whiter thanks to all the sun he got on his face today. "And besides, last night left me kinda thirsty for *nonalcoholic* beverages."

We *did* wake up quite hung over. "Point taken." Nonetheless, we sit at the bar so we can watch the Sox game on the widescreen television.

"I don't think I've seen you fine men in here before." I'm out of practice with the ladies, but there's no doubt in my mind that the approaching dark-haired girl is flirting.

Right before she starts to purr, her blonde friend adds, "I don't know about you, but *I'd* remember these guys."

Just like that, we're surrounded. And the purring—it's loud. Loud enough to be heard above the racket of the game, which is on surround sound. Maybe I'm exaggerating, but she still sounds like a horny tigress.

I'm embarrassed to admit I hadn't even noticed there were girls in the bar, but they hadn't missed us. The shiny-lipped blue-eyed blonde and her sultry, dark-haired purring friend are suddenly too close. And they have the same look in their eyes as Mom does when she's shopping for sweaters at The Wilson Bargain Basement. *Which one do I prefer? And which would look better on me?*

Liam is a complete gentleman. He quickly stands and offers his stool. Reluctantly, I do the same. After an exchanged glance, the two girls switch places; they seem to have wordlessly decided that the dark-haired one is to be mine and the blonde is for Liam. They sit and cross their legs as the bartender approaches.

"Can we buy you ladies a couple of drinks?" Liam asks.

Does he ask this smoothly? Politely? It's hard to say, but it hits me that Liam could very well be a ladies' man, and my chest starts to pound. I pat all around the tiny pocket on the front of my T-shirt in search of a racing heartbeat. I feel nothing—my heart has gone missing... So there's no danger of it breaking.

"Why thank you. I could go for a Long Island iced tea," says blondie, as she further unbuttons her already *very* unbuttoned, snug purple blouse. My gaze, along with that of Liam and the bartender, slides into the deep crevice.

"Make that two Long Islands. And, Missy, I think your handsome hunk likes what he sees," the dark-haired girl chimes in with a husky chuckle, nodding at Liam's wide eyes.

Handsome hunk. It has a certain ring...and I don't like it.

"You boys aren't drinking?" Liam's girl observes, placing one delicate hand over her shiny O-shaped lips.

"Missy Rose, shut up. They probably belong to AA, or something." She lowers her voice, pokes a pointy jet-black nail into my face, and asks gently, "Are you guys alcoholics, or what?"

Strangely intimidated, I can think of no direct or indirect way of answering her.

Liam is quick with a comeback. "No. We just had too much to drink last night and so we're taking it easy tonight."

"So, you got a girlfriend?" She stares into my eyes. When I don't answer, she asks, "Don't you understand plain English—I just wanna know if you're dating somebody?"

I see Ginny in my head. Her long dreads are tucked up under a black beanie, and her face is flushed with what she called "intolerance with the world's fucking ignorance." And this ghost of Ginny is rolling her eyes and shaking her head.

I know exactly what she's thinking: *You for real, Jase? You gonna go and get horizontal with this smart ass who thinks she's all that?*

Liam steps up beside me, and one of his massive arms encircles my shoulders. "He's recently lost an important relationship in his life." I think you could call this being saved by the bell. "So what we're having here is a *guys'* night out."

"Well, that sounds like fun!!" Liam's girl reminds me of the cheerleaders in high school. She pumps her arms as if shouting, "Go, team, go!"

"Hmmm..." Lola is deep in thought. "I know how to take your mind off your broken heart. It's my specialty." She sticks her finger into the pocket of my T-shirt, pokes it down deep, and then seductively pulls it out. "I'm Lola, and she's Missy Rose. Some people call us the Bourne Hospitality Club."

I reach out to shake Lola's hand, but she has something different in mind. She pops off of the bar stool, and next thing I know, I'm wearing her like a ski jacket.

Liam steps back and shakes Missy Rose's perfect little pale fingers that happen to be decorated with bubblegum-pink nail polish, complete with tiny sparkle-roses. "I'm Liam, and this is my buddy, Jase. And as I said, it's a *guys'* night out."

"*Jase*...hmmm? I *adore* that name...oh, shit... Jayzee! Jay Zee! Jay Zeeeeeee!" Lola, who's already drunk off her fine ass, lifts her drink from the bar and swigs down at least half in a single gulp. If she didn't belch so loudly afterward, it would have been impressive. "They put way too much fucking ice in these things!" She swirls the remaining liquid around in the glass and then looks past it at me. "Want a sip?"

I shake my head. "Uh...no, thank you."

Where Lola is drunk as a skunk, Missy Rose is coy. *And* she's skilled at playing the sexy card. "So, Mr. Muscles...you have *got* to be the best-built man in this place." She flashes her eyes and reaches up to pinch Liam's biceps. "How much can you bench-press? Don't be shy...tell sweet Missy Rose."

Sweet? I don't think so.

Liam and I are by now wide-eyed, slightly revolted, and I can't speak for him, but I'm intimidated by their feminine fierceness. When Liam and I look at each other, we can't help but burst into a fit of nervous laughter.

"What's so funny, assholes?" Lola doesn't care to be laughed at. "College guys think they're God's gift to classy young ladies like me and Missy here!"

"Lola, calm down, they're just trying to have a good time." Missy Rose strokes Liam's chest. Soon her fingernails are sliding his black suspenders right off his shoulders. "I can show you a *better* time than a boys' night, Liam...if you give me half a chance."

All of a sudden this isn't fun anymore. Liam is staring down into Missy Rose's face and smiling, which twists my guts. Maybe his smile *is* as uncomfortable as a pig in a bacon bits packaging plant, but it's a smile nonetheless. And Lola appears pissed off and at the same time horny as hell, and she actually has the balls to grab for mine.

Liam is in her face in less than a split second. "Hands off, lady." He doesn't shout. He doesn't lay a finger on her, although he looks as if he wants to. He steps up between us, which is a challenge because Lola's still on me like snug outerwear, and informs her that I'm unavailable. "He's with me."

I've been claimed.

By a guy.

And how do I feel about this?

Mostly I'm relieved. Especially when Lola screams, "You guys are nothing but puke stains! And you're teases—leading us on like that when you're a couple?"

But is a feeling of *relief* enough to do what we're apparently now doing—leaving this pub together, arm in arm?

Chapter Nine

SITTING IN LIAM'S car in the parking lot of the Beachcomber Bar and Grille, we stare in opposite directions out the open side windows.

"I'm sorry. I was totally out of line back there." As usual, Liam speaks first. He's definitely the icebreaker in this relationship.

"What do you mean, *out of line*?"

"Maybe you wanted to get busy with Lady Lola of Trash-Mouth Mountain, and I blew it for you."

I laugh. "You didn't blow anything for me, Liam. Lady Lola actually scares me. But hot little Missy Rose...she sure has a thing for you. I think you were destined for an evening of wild sexual fun and games...but you had to step in and save my pearly-white ass." I lean toward him so that I can nudge him with my elbow. "Not that I'm counting, but now you've saved me three times, huh?"

"Missy Rose isn't my type." Liam doesn't laugh, and he holds his shoulders high and stiff, more awkward than I've ever seen him. "Let's get outta here."

He starts the car and speeds south on Shore Road.

"I had a vision of Ginny when we were in the pub," I tell him as he drives.

"You did?"

"Yeah. And she wasn't pleased with the kind of girl who was trying to hook up with me." Liam cracks a smile, and I'm relieved. "Ginny always thought *she* was the only one allowed to get away with excessive profanity."

He is starting to relax. "I thought *I* ruined your chance of getting laid."

"Really, Liam? You know me pretty well by now. Does Lola *really* seem like my kind of girl?"

He doesn't hesitate. "Not at all." And even though it's getting dark, I can tell he's blushing. "She's pretty much the polar opposite of how I see you."

"And how *do* you see me?" I can't believe I ask him this, and from the way his jaw drops, neither can he.

He doesn't say anything until he pulls into the first casual restaurant we come across. "Let's see if there's a long wait for dinner."

I can't believe he ignored my question. Liam's not a mean-spirited person, and I want to know why he completely blew me off. But I'm not one to push an issue, so I decide to bide my time. "Sounds good to me."

Once we're settled on bar stools, I hope he'll start explaining. Why did he *need* to go on this trip with me, like he said on the day he invited me to come along? And what does he see when he looks at me? Answers to these questions would clue me in on Liam's motivation to help me. But Liam explains nothing, and we end up talking about the problems the Red Sox must overcome if they want to be contenders next year.

I'm an avoider of all things controversial, and Liam is a secret keeper. Neither of us seems particularly willing to do what's necessary to change this status.

BACK AT THE cottage, we grab a six-pack of beer, snap on the television, and again retreat to the oversized floral couch, tonight sitting shoulder to shoulder rather than on opposite ends. *Is this an instant replay of last night?* I'm not sure if that's what I want.

After forty-five minutes of beer drinking and small talk—favorite sports teams, bands we've seen live, dorm room assignments for next year— we're buzzed and starting to relax. And I feel daring.

Daring is not an adjective I'd normally use to describe myself. The most daring things I've ever done actually all involve going along with the grand schemes of other people. *Following them. Daring* is simply not how I'm programmed. But tonight I step out of my comfort zone; I'm not sure what I hope to accomplish. Strangely, I do it anyway.

"You never told me if you have a girlfriend." My cheeks burn with embarrassment at having made such a bold statement.

He looks at me very directly. The blond spikes on top of his head are doing that slumping-to-the-left thing they do at night, and his expression has lost some of its sharpness. "You never asked."

"Well, I just did."

"I'm not sure there's a clear-cut answer." He turns toward me and lifts an arm to the back of the couch.

"Tell me anyway." I've never been so persistent in acquiring the information I want from a reluctant person. Usually, I let people unfold at their own pace, allowing them to tell me what they want me to know. "Just say it."

"I'm much better at showing than telling."

And with those cryptic words, where he fully avoids the subject of his dating life, he leans forward and kisses me squarely on the lips. It's a chaste kiss but filled with the promise of more that will be far less innocent. He pauses, probably waiting to see if I'll punch him out or shove him away because he made a move. And when I do neither—not because the urge to shove him is absent, but because I'm so tangled in confusion regarding my sexual orientation—he places his hands on either side of my face and leans forward to kiss me again.

This time his kiss is soft and moist and unrushed. He pulls back just slightly before he cocks his head and comes at my mouth from a different angle. I have no idea if I'm responding or if I'm merely doing what I do best: riding the wave. Thoughts of Ginny, of Lola, and of the first girl I kissed in grade school behind the baseball dugout, swirl around like hurricane winds in my mind. And when I notice the scratch of his beard against my chin, the single word *gay* surfaces in my brain.

Gay...

I've never before seen myself this way. Even the night he got me off at the hotel hadn't made me feel as gay as sharing this kiss with Liam. I'm not sure why I want to deny it, but I can't— Tonight, at least, I want to keep going in this direction. And in the morning, I'll likely blame my actions on booze or trauma or the loss of my girlfriend or a serious case of hero worship, or on anything that comes to mind when I decide it's time to make my straight escape. But, right now I need to go along with this. I lift my hands to the sides of his beard and pull him closer.

Liam establishes his dominance the very instant I let him know that our kiss is okay with me. To be honest, his control of this situation thrills me in a way I quickly realize could be a game changer. The abandon with which he's kissing me now—the sureness and direction and desire he's struggling to reign in—leads me into pleasure, without allowing for the kind of second thoughts or doubts that have previously inhibited me. He leads, I follow. It actually *is* that simple.

I've never felt comfortable in the sexually aggressive role that's expected of me as a "red-blooded American man." I struggled with Ginny to find the place I wanted to be when in bed. But Liam seems to already know this, as I'm currently living my secret passive fantasy in his arms.

"Lie flat beneath me and be still," Liam says when our passionate kiss finally comes to its breathy conclusion. "Because I want to take in every inch of you, and I can see you better when your body isn't moving so much. You will do this for me?"

I'm surprised at how easy it is to lower my eyes and nod.

Liam pushes me down flat on the bold, flowery fabric and studies my fully clothed body. I can't remove my gaze from his face, as he's so totally absorbed in me. The hunger I see is more than flattering; it's addictive. Then, without a hint of hesitation, he reaches for the hem of my T-shirt and, with a glance, enlists my cooperation as he pulls it cleanly over my head. My chest is bare and exposed and I feel vulnerable. I try to cross my arms in front of me, but Liam pushes them to my sides. When his lips, surrounded by the scruffy bush of his beard, brush the skin on my ribcage, the rush of arousal makes me gasp.

"Stay still...and take what I give you." Liam pins my arms to the couch and proceeds to feast on my chest. When I feel his sharp teeth nibbling on one nipple, then the other, I begin to writhe and forget the very last of my reservations.

"You're mine...I saved you, and now it's my job to take care of the big stuff *and* the small stuff— everything you need. No one's gonna hurt you or scare you... I won't let anybody harm so much as a hair on your head, Jase...I won't." Liam rambles on and on—vows of how he'll protect me— as he unbuttons and then unzips my jeans. As soon as the fly is open, he slides his hand inside and cups my balls.

I struggle a bit with the awareness that it's a man's hand on me, but this doesn't diminish my erection. "You're gonna be mine and you're gonna know it tonight." His face drops down below my waist, and first, he nuzzles my entire crotch— he's breathing me in—and then he mouths the tip of my dick through the thin cotton of my boxers.

I gasp again at the blissful sensation and the knowledge that a man is giving it to me. "I've never felt like this..." I speak with complete honesty; I've never felt this turned on, even with Ginny. My come-clean candor surprises me because it *so* isn't my style. "What now? What comes next?"

Liam lifts his face from between my legs, and he smiles. My discomfort seems to give him confidence, as well as to feed his passion, and he replies, "All good things, Jase. *Only good things.*"

I lift my ass more eagerly than I can believe so he's able to easily pull down my shorts, and when they're on the floor beside us, he bites the elastic of my boxers and tugs at them with his teeth. I reach down to help him pull them off, but Liam's huge palm stops me. "I want to undress you myself. Stay still."

Complying is easy, freeing, and exactly what I want. He reaches for the waistband of my boxers and peels them down quickly, causing my dick to pop up, right into his face. For just a moment, his action seems experimental; he licks the moisture at the tip and hums as if the flavor is unique and wonderful, like nothing else he's tasted. His reaction is unexpected and stimulating.

The contrast of being naked when Liam is fully dressed further fuels my arousal; I feel helpless to the desire of the man beside me. I begin to tremble, not from cold, but from the awareness that I'm not the one in control. I must wait— completely still—until he chooses to move this experience forward.

"Keep your hands by your sides," Liam orders gently as he releases my arms. He then proceeds to examine my stiff dick, and I want desperately to cover myself, but Liam is the king tonight, and he wants to do things his way. This is how it will be.

"Have you ever been sucked by a man?" His attention shifts from my dick to my eyes. When I shake my head, he says, "Neither have I, but I know what feels good. So, I'd say you're gonna need to brace yourself."

His words alone send a spasm of chills up my spine. I clutch the flowery fabric on the couch in my fists as Liam roughly parts my legs and climbs between them. His shoulders are broad, and the fit on the couch is tight, but that doesn't deter him. He bends down and without a second of hesitation swallows me wholly and enthusiastically. Nothing has ever felt this good. I'm not sure anything ever will.

After sucking with rapt determination and bringing me to the edge three times, Liam pulls his own T-shirt off, and I'm presented with the ripped muscles of a man who possesses true physical superiority over most everyone he meets.

A man...a man...

He reaches down to unbutton his own fly, and he pulls out his dick. It's enormous and hard and as eager as I am for what will come next.

"I can't wait any longer," he tells me with urgency, and before I know it, he's again bent between my thighs. "I want you to arch your back when you come, and then I'm going to get up on my knees and finish myself off. I'm gonna come on your skin." He's staring up at me again, trying to talk without gasping for air. One of his hands is hard at work on his own dick, and I reach out to touch his face, but he says, "Hands at your sides, please."

My entire body quivers as I place my hands by my sides, close my eyes, and accept how he pulls assertively on my dick with his tongue. In less than thirty seconds, I reach down to touch Liam's shoulder, giving him the signal that it's time.

"I want to see." His voice is raspy, and he lifts his head to watch me come, my back arched in ecstasy as he requested. The instant I lower my back to the couch, he kneels and jerks himself—once, twice, and then his warm come is splashing on my belly.

Within a minute he's up off the couch, leading me to the bedroom, where he cleans me with his T-shirt and pulls me into bed.

Chapter Ten

CAN TWO MEN experience emotional and sexual satisfaction with each other when they aren't gay?

I wake up with this question on my mind.

It was already over, romantically speaking, with Ginny when the shooting took place in the theater. Ginny and I had agreed that we'd spend the summer apart and when we returned from break, it would be as friends. I was too tame to fit her idea of "the perfect man," and my feelings for Ginny had shifted over time from romantic love to deep admiration. And though our impending breakup was by mutual agreement, it had still been difficult for me to accept. But there's no doubt, I'd once loved Ginny and had been fulfilled by our relationship. *How can I possibly feel so complete this morning, after having been possessed in bed by a man?*

To be honest, last night with Liam I experienced a kind of sexual satisfaction I was unaware even existed.

But, shit, *I loved Ginny.* I wanted her body and I treasured her brain and I found her to be the funniest, quirkiest, most fascinating person I'd ever met. I *loved* her, for Christ's sake. *So I must be straight.* I only ever dated girls in the past; I took girls to proms and homecoming dances and down by the lake to make out and home to meet my mother. I've never looked at the masculine form—a scruffy beard, massive thighs, a deep voice, ripped pecs, a powerful back—and experienced sexual desire.

With one fucking humongous exception. And right now he's draped on top of me, literally. Lying on his belly on the double bed, his sturdy arm is stretched across my hips, his legs entwined with mine. We're both naked, and I'm hard as a rock, the quandary regarding my sexual orientation doing nothing to diminish my morning wood.

"You're up." He pulls my body tight and his palm comes down on my erection.

"In more ways than one," I quip.

"I'll take care of it for you." His hand begins to move as his mouth finds the hollow of my neck, and the feel of his scratchy beard, contrasted with his soft lips on my throat, along with the steady pumping of my dick, has me coming immediately. He watches closely as I arch my body against his. *Yeah...I do it again, as I know he liked it when I did it last night. When did I become such a pleaser?*

I've never touched a man with the intention of pleasuring him, and the mere thought sends me into a state of bewilderment. It's amazing how a morning orgasm can make you see the big picture so clearly. Liam senses my sudden reluctance, and when I awkwardly reach for his dick, he takes my hand in his and kisses it, then excuses himself to the shower.

Part of me wants to trail after him—I'm a committed follower—but the rest of me isn't so sure it's the right thing to do. I'm out of my league here; I don't know what any of this *means*. I just know he makes me happy in a way I've never been happy before, but I doubt it can really be that simple. How can Liam perform so well sexually with me, another guy?

Maybe he's bi.

He's about the manliest man I've ever met, and I always thought that possessing masculinity meant a guy had to be straight and… Right now, the subject of sexual orientation clearly confuses me and upsets me to a degree.

I decide to make toast.

WE SHARE ANOTHER awesome day together, swimming and sunbathing on the tiny beach in front of the cottage. All day, I fight the urge to touch him. But more than that, I struggle with the desire for Liam to touch me. I want him to push me down on the sand and do whatever he wants to my body, but he's as wary as I am. Neither of us is the world's best communicator, and because we're driving home later this afternoon, there's no way we can drink beer to loosen our lips.

After we go out to lunch at a bagel shop, we head back to our cozy little cottage. And despite the fact that I'm unsure of what I'm doing—I have no clue what this *thing* is between Liam and me—I just can't fight my urge to connect with him, *really* connect with him, one more time before we part.

"Shit, I'm beat. You up for a nap?" I have no idea if he buys my fake exhaustion, so I yawn to better sell it.

The way he looks at me breaks my heart. In this man, I see more fear than I saw on his face in that dark theater last April.

"You sure it's what you want?" He's giving me a chance to back out of what I just offered. He glances away as he awaits my answer.

"I want to." And Jase, the follower, leads Liam into the cottage.

We go straight to the bedroom, where the sheets are rumpled and the blanket is pooled up at the end of the bed, just the way we left them this morning. Liam and I climb onto the bed and lie flat on our backs, so close our shoulders touch.

"I'm still sandy from the beach." He speaks in a listless monotone.

"So am I. A little sand won't hurt us."

"'Kay." I turn toward him and admit the truth. "I'm not gay." I hear him sigh, longer and louder than usual. "I'm not gay, but I feel things for you I can't explain."

Apparently my second brief confession is sufficient to set Liam at ease. He wraps his arms around me, and once again, I experience a measure of peace and contentment, as well as a feeling of being bonded in a way that can't be broken.

"I've never been with a guy, but I wanna make love to you, Jase. I'm not sure what this makes me, sexually speaking, and I'm pretty sure I don't care." Liam doesn't dance around it. "I can make this something you'll never forget. Let me."

I nod. I want this. I want to feel the way I felt last night. But still my mind races with questions about my sexuality and his sexuality, and Liam knows it.

"Sshhh. Settle down. It's gonna be okay."

He's right. When I'm with him, everything's okay. He's proved this time and again. *He's my hero, isn't he?* So I nod again, and then I settle down as he told me to do. And I wait for what comes next.

"Maybe we should rinse off in the shower. There *are* some things sand *will* hurt."

AS I STAND under the stream of water, I again think about Ginny. I remember the first time we made love; she had been an unlikely virgin. Her outer image was so cool and "whatever, dude" that I almost didn't believe her when she told me she'd never before "gone all the way." I tried to make the first time memorable for her, as I'm sure Liam wants to do for me. With Ginny, I'd felt pressure, though, to perform and to satisfy and to be aggressive enough but not too much, and all in all, the experience was more stressful than satisfying.

I wonder if Liam feels similar pressure or if, because we're both guys, first times somehow aren't as noteworthy.

After we rinse our bodies of sand, we return to the bedroom, still damp and naked from the shower. We stand here staring at each other until he urges, "Lie down on your stomach. I wanna rub your back 'til you're relaxed."

To relax me? Under the circumstances, it might take quite a lot of effort—Liam could still be rubbing my back at six tonight—but I flip onto my belly anyway. "Okay."

He climbs on my ass, bends in half, and speaks softly into my ear. "I'm gonna rub your shoulders really hard. It might hurt a little, but when I'm done you're gonna feel like a..."

And suddenly I'm back... I'm back on the floor of the theater with Liam's weight pressing me into the seats, protecting me from being shot. I'm terrified and sweating, and at the same time, I'm frozen. He whispers into my ear, "I'm gonna push on your back really hard and I want you to squeeze as much of your body underneath the chairs as you can, got it?"

I squeeze my eyes shut. "I can't do this again...no...not again!"

The room is dark...pitch black...all I can do is absorb the fear and hear the—

Pop-pop-pop...pop-pop-pop...

"Ginny...I'm sorry, Ginny...I lost you...I let you die!"

Pop-pop-pop...

"Liam...where are you, Liam? Liam!"

Pop-pop-pop...

"Hey, Jase...Jase...it's okay. I'm here..." But he's a million miles away.

My breathing is ragged...I have to control it. Small breaths...short breaths...

"No more short breaths, 'kay? You'll faint...you need to breathe deep. Do it with me."

"He'll see... Liam, if I breathe deep, my chest will rise and I'll make your body move and he'll see and he'll kill you..."

"One...two...three...nice and slow...breathe with me..."

Against my better judgment, I do as he says, but as soon as my breathing slows down, the comforting weight slips from my back, and I'm cold and alone and exposed.

Pop-pop-pop...

"Liam!"

"Jason, you're safe...you're with me at the cottage...and we spent the day swimming in the bay, remember? I won't let him hurt you...not ever." There's a hand in mine and it's huge and strong...and a beard scratching the back of my neck. "Open your eyes...you'll see that you're safe."

I trust the voice in my ear...I really do. If he says to open my eyes, I should open them. When I finally take a peek at the world, I see one thing—one person— and it's all I need. "Liam..."

"Look around...check out where we are."

We're in a dingy old bedroom of a salty-smelling cottage with a view of the ocean out the open window.

"You're okay, and Dom DeSalles is dead. He's never coming back and, besides, now you have me to watch out for you."

Just like that, I'm in the cottage again...and I'm humiliated. I want to cry, but I'm determined to stop the tears that have welled up in my eyes from spilling down my cheeks. "I'm sorry...this has happened to me at home but it's never happened when I'm out."

"It's all right...I think you had a flashback. No worries at all. I'm just glad I could be here for you."

I turn toward him and hug him tight. "We were about to...to *do something*...weren't we?" The dreamy romantic energy between us is lost, but I'm willing to try to retrieve it.

"If you don't mind, I think I'll just hold you for a while."

Without letting go, I say, "Holding me is just what I think we both need and...and it looks as if you saved me...again."

"It is my life's greatest goal." He says it with a smile and a wink, but I can tell he's not joking.

Part Three

August

Chapter Eleven

MY BEDROOM IS hot and stuffy as the screen in the window above my bed tore the first time I forced the stubborn window open this summer, and, in order not to invite in bugs, I'm forced to keep it closed. There's no cross-ventilation, and it feels like a late-August sauna in here, but I continue to pack my boxers and socks neatly into a rolling suitcase. This less-than-demanding task has left me with the solitude I've been avoiding since I returned from Cape Cod. A perfectly unwelcome environment if you want to avoid thinking.

After my short trip to Cape Cod, I improved psychologically, and I did so rapidly. Therapy sessions became incredibly useful, where before they were exercises in futility. I got in touch with my friends from high school, Kendrick and Dan; we went to a Red Sox game, a couple of hometown barbeques, and swimming in the local reservoir. I've even made an effort with Mom so she knows I'm on the path to recovery, despite the fact she never really listens to much I say.

And I visited Ginny's parents. We grieved together. It was painful but brought about some closure for all of us.

I've been eating and sleeping regularly, and sometimes I hit the gym. And even if I'm not planning on going to the theater any time soon, I'm a different guy than I was before I went away with Liam. In a good way. I have no clue why I improved so much after I came back from Cape Cod. And I try not to ask too many questions because it was a good thing that had something to do with me finding hope. The only problem is, although I have new hope for the future, I'm not sure I like the guy I've become.

And because I know I'm going to see Liam in the next few days, as we're going to be living in the same dormitory again, I finally level with myself. I used Liam to again rescue me from my life at the sludgy bottom of the barrel, which was where it had ended up by mid-July of summer break when he whisked me off to Cape Cod. I took just enough from him to gain the sense of hope for the future I needed to rejoin the world of the living. Once I had that precious hope, I tucked it against my chest and ran with it, refusing to acknowledge I got it from him and thinking I could pretend it was mine all along. But the new mentally stable Jason isn't even close to being as genuine as the terrified, needy one who went away for a weekend with the friend from college who'd saved my life, time and again.

But as I said, I don't ask too many questions. Closely examining the ins and outs, the why's and why not's—it's just not who I am.

To sum it up, I haven't stayed in contact with Liam. He has my cell number and used it a few times to check on me. Likewise, I have his number, but I never returned his calls. I heard the calls come in, waited as they rang, and watched as they went to voicemail. Where they've remained, never having been listened to. And I've sat alone on my bed a hundred times, *a thousand times*, staring at the cell phone on my desk, wanting so badly to dial his number. But I've never followed through.

I'm not sure of the exact reason for my inaction—maybe it's because Liam reminds me of the violence and terror I want to forget, but more likely, it's a personal sexuality issue. When I think about him, I first get warm and soon hot, my stomach tightens and my throat grows an enormous lump. Then I start to feel vulnerable because, not only has Liam seen me at my lowest point, he's taken me to my highest with his hand and his mouth and his simple words. I'm caught in an awkward place between wanting him, needing him, and feeling compelled to reject him, because *I am not gay* and what Liam represents is a totally new kind of life that I'm not sure I can embrace. And no, I'm not homophobic... This whole *having sexual, not to mention romantic, feelings for the man who saved my life* thing has taken me by surprise, that's all.

I'm pretty sure my avoidance of Liam has much more to do with sexuality issues than unwanted reminders of the shooting.

I'm a coward.

In any case, I've gotten together a few times with my high school girlfriend, Carrie Dodd, and I won't lie, our single attempt at hooking up felt more wrong than right...more disappointing than sweet. The best way I can describe it is "I got the job done," but even that's a lie because I didn't. *Nobody* finished, to put it politely. Still, I've done my best to roll with it...with her. Carrie's gorgeous and sexy and reasonably intelligent. Being with her doesn't require me to think too hard or question myself, and I'm cool with that part.

I'm normal Jason Tripp again, right?

I'm the guy I was before I met Ginny—the first girl to make me laugh and think and look at the world in a different way—and before I was nearly shot in the head...on two different occasions. And before I was touched by the hand and the heart of a man who I simultaneously crave and abhor.

Sure, I'm normal Jase...

Mom peeks her head into my bedroom. "I think that's all of it, dear. I have your clothes pressed and folded into the two large duffel bags, and I baked enough double-chocolate fudge brownies for you to share with your entire floor. They're in my green-and-white Tupperware containers—and I want the containers back, you hear me? Tupperware doesn't grow on trees."

Mom has gradually come to accept that I'm returning to Batcheldor College to continue my study of journalism. I'm glad to be returning. I need some space from her. The woman is great in many ways, but suffocating too. "Thanks, Mom."

"That poor sweet Carrie seemed so dejected when she left here this morning. I hope you plan on staying in touch with her. She would make me an excellent daughter-in-law."

I cough twice and then get myself together enough to offer my mother a noncommittal shrug. When Mom sends me a stern glance, I smile innocently, and then I shake my head so she knows Carrie isn't a permanent fixture in my life.

"Good girls like her don't grow on trees, either, young man."

It's far more likely that I'll hang on to the green-and-white Tupperware containers for the long haul than I'll hold onto Carrie, so I shake my head again. "I think it's time we head to Vermont." Sometimes changing the subject is the only way out of these types of unwanted heart-to-hearts with Mom. "Jack, the head of club soccer at school, expects me to be back in time for the team meetings."

Mom smiles, and it's genuine. "Well, keep in mind that if a certain soccer player invited a certain mother to watch a soccer game or two, she wouldn't say no."

"Not subtle, Mom. But I'll let you know when I get my game schedule."

I receive a quick squeeze before she heads for our minivan's driver's seat.

"Mom, I can drive back to school."

She shakes her head with something close to vehemence. "The way you apply the brakes makes me ill. Now get your bottom into the passenger seat and buckle your seat belt."

I can't argue with that, and like a kid, I'm driven away to college in our family minivan for the second time in as many years.

I WONDERED IF I would freak out when we drove past the Harrison Theater on our way to RetroHouse, but I didn't. I just held my head stiffly and stared straight in front of me, allowing residual numbness to envelop me.

Now, I'm in my new dormitory room that's slightly bigger than my basement room of last year, and on the main floor, as well. Mom made my bed—it'll probably never be made again this year, not that she needs to know this—and unpacked my freshly ironed clothing into the standard issue bureau. She was most excited to pass out her brownies to anyone and everyone on my floor.

I find myself eager for her to leave so that I can go upstairs to where most of the seniors are housed and look for Liam before the soccer meeting. I've been surprisingly obsessed by this desire, and the very second Mom leaves, I bolt for the stairs.

Seniors all have large single rooms—the reward for three long years of sharing space with roommates. I walk down the long hall on the fourth floor and read the nametags on each door, none of which have *Liam Norcross* printed neatly across its width. This is odd; when we were in the summer cottage, he told me he was going to be living in the senior singles in RetroHouse this year.

I'm left with no choice but to ask someone where he's living. So I linger in the hallway until a hipster dude saunters out of his room, and I call out, "Hey...excuse me, I have a question."

He looks at me strangely, probably wondering what on earth a lowly underclassman is doing on the senior floor. "Yeah?"

"Do you know Liam Norcross? He's supposed to be living up here, and I don't see a room with his name on it."

"Norcross bailed on living in RetroHouse at the last minute. I'm the lucky dude who got his room. As far as I know, he got a place off campus."

I'm surprised—no, make that fucking shocked. And hurt...but I'm not sure exactly why. "Do you know where his apartment is?"

"Do I *look* like a frigging address book?" He walks past me to the stairs. "Get a life."

"Maybe I'll do that..." I utter, stunned. It's as if I've been slapped hard in the face. Not only does Liam refuse to live in the same dormitory as me, but he also didn't tell me about his change in plans.

I know...I know...I never returned his calls. But still...

Chapter Twelve

I CAN'T FIND him.

He doesn't answer or return my phone calls, but I can't complain since it's exactly what I did to him last summer. I already went to the Registrar's Office and asked for his new address, but the secretary told me she couldn't disclose that information. I never knew who his roommate was—or any of his friends—but I do know he'd gone to see Ginny's roommate, Mariah Craft, perform on the night of the theater shootings. It doesn't take much of a detective to figure out where she's living. The sophomores are housed in RetroHouse and Hamilton Hall, and since she isn't living in my dorm, I stop by Hamilton Hall at the end of the first day of classes.

It's the bad kind of déjà vu. I pace up and down the halls of the girls' floors in Hamilton Hall, reading the names posted on the doors of the young women who live here, and I don't see Mariah's name. I'm forced to camp out in the lobby until a girl I recognize enters the dorm.

"Hi...your name's Emily, right?" I've never before put myself out there this way. But I really want to find Liam.

"Yeah...weren't you...uh, Ginny Blankenship's boyfriend?" She seems to realize how stupid a thing it is to ask halfway through saying it.

"Yeah...that's me." Ginny would likely have been living in this very hallway if she hadn't been killed last spring. For a moment, my eyes sting—it hurts to think about Ginny. But

I pull myself together because I'm on a mission. "Do you know which room is Mariah Craft's? I haven't talked to her since...last spring and...I want to say hi."

"Oh, you don't know?" With flashing blue eyes and wavy, light brown hair, the girl is classically hot. I recognize this but feel no interest or attraction.

"Know what?"

"Mariah transferred out of Batcheldor College over the summer. She couldn't deal with what happened to...you know, to Ginny...and she's going to school somewhere in Massachusetts now."

"Mariah's gone?"

Emily nods. "I can probably track down somebody who has her number."

I'm getting no closer to finding Liam. "I...I think I can figure out how to reach Mariah. But thanks, anyway." Without waiting for a response, I race down the hallway and out of the building.

If I want to find Liam Norcross, I'm going to have to bump into him on campus by chance.

Chapter Thirteen

I HAVE THE same roommate as last year, BJ Landon. He's a good guy and was especially cool after the theater shooting. He packed all of my stuff in our dorm room into cardboard boxes and loaded them into Mom's minivan so I wouldn't have to come back to school and face things I wasn't ready for.

But BJ is wild. W.I.L.D. And sure, I like to have a good time, but I'm not all about crashing into my bed—or on the floor in the vicinity of my bed, as is often the case for BJ—in a drunken stupor. Every night of the week.

It's the first weekend and BJ is growing crazier by the minute. Until now, I've steered clear of parties, as my attitude toward learning, and maybe even toward life in general, is much changed from last year. I'm a more serious and focused person now. But BJ pretty much begged me to hang out with him tonight—there are three keg parties in RetroHouse *alone* that he knows of, and a late-night pizza bash with some freshman girls in the basement.

I want to be excited about the parties and the pizza and the girls, and to be lighthearted like BJ. I want to be the uncomplicated college student I thought I could again be. But the feeling of apathy I've experienced over the past week regarding welcome-back parties and crazy coeds lets me know I'm not able to pass for a fun, easygoing guy.

"You've been hitting the books too hard this week, Jase. And you know what they say about all work and no play, don't you?"

I laugh. "It makes Jase a dull boy, but also a boy with straight A's."

"Here, drink this." BJ hands me a shot of something amber, and even though I'm not in the mood, I suck it down. Apparently, I'm still something of a follower. "Now, word is out that you've been searching for some senior dude. What's the deal with that?"

It's true that I put the word out this week. I did everything short of hanging signs on trees that say *LOST: One Valiant Hero* to let the Batcheldor community know I'm looking for Liam Norcross. I'm still not exactly sure what I'm going to say to him, but I know I need to see him. Badly. *Obsessively badly.* "The deal is that I want to see the guy who saved my butt last year."

I now have BJ's undivided attention. "This Norcross dude saved you? That night in the Harrison Theater?"

The police know what Liam did for me, but the details haven't gone viral on campus. "Yeah. And I need to talk to him."

"Sure as shit you do! And after you guys talk, you gotta get him bombed off his ass, that's what you need to do! You owe him big time."

"I just want to talk to him, that's all."

This first week back to school has been almost as hard for me as the week after the shootings, which seems to be a dramatic claim, but it's true. I thought being back in the college environment might tear me apart because of the reminders of Ginny and of all the violence and death of last spring. But what's tearing me apart is knowing I messed everything up with Liam because I was confused...because I wasn't ready to see myself as bisexual, or possibly gay.

"Well, I know a few seniors, and I'll tell them to kidnap him and deliver him to our dorm room, then we can treat him to one hell of a rowdy night— I can pick up some weed— and we can cap it all off with a freshman girl *happy ending!*"

I sigh, but the sound is yet another reminder of Liam. *Why didn't I return his calls?* I must be crazy—my retreat from Liam this summer just doesn't make sense. After one of the best weekends of my life, where I turned a major corner and began to recover from emotional devastation, I literally pretended that the person who gave me this peace of mind didn't exist.

"Not a good idea, BJ. I don't think kidnapping him would be much of a thank-you."

"Here." He hands me another shot. "Down the hatch, dude."

And this is how I end up getting wasted. Just talking nonsense with BJ, sucking down shots between lines of stupid chitchat. Within an hour, I follow BJ out the doorway of our dorm room, on our way to the first of three keg parties.

BY THE TIME we hit the third party, all I want is to go crash in my bed. And for the room not to be spinning. Maybe not in that order.

"Dude—I found myself a pretty friend to keep me company tonight!" BJ is plastered to this cute little red-haired girl. He already has the top button of her jeans undone from what I can see. "Listen, Tripp, me and Dacia need the room...so you gotta find yourself another place to crash tonight." He glances down at his tiny, carrot-top conquest. "We're gonna be real busy..."

"Wait up, BJ! I...I got nowhere to go!" I'm drunk and exhausted and way too dizzy for comfort.

"Hit up those freshman girls in the basement. They'll let ya sleep on their floor. It's room B-12." BJ is every bit as smashed as I am, but he's motivated by birds and bees and Dacia's come-hither smile. "Good luck, dude!"

I slide to the floor and grab the edge of a nearby plant pot for steadiness. This is going to be a long night.

IT'S TWO IN the morning, and for all intents and purposes, I'm homeless.

"Hey, kid, you gotta vacate the premises. In other words—take a hike. My room ain't a bed-and-breakfast." I recognize the voice. It's the same hipster senior who told me that he had no clue where Liam is living this year.

All I can do is moan. I'm literally sick and tired.

"Hey, Liam, do you know this kid? He was here looking for you last week, but I had no frigging idea where you lived...in fact, I still don't, so send me an email with your addy." Hipster-guy laughs. "It's late, and I want the kid to get the hell outta here. Don't want him to get sick in my plant pot."

"*Liam?*" It's the only word he says that makes sense. "Liam..."

And then Liam is beside me, lifting me, holding me beneath my shoulders. "Jason...which dorm room is yours?"

I don't answer. I can't.

"Get him the hell out of here. All I need is to get caught with a drunk underage student in my place." Hipster-guy yells, and Liam leads me down the hall and toward the stairs.

"*Your dorm room, Jason?* Which one is it?" Liam's impatient. I get a sense he wants to cut and run but is too honorable to dump me in a stairwell.

"Can't go to my room. BJ is getting a B.J." This hits me as inexplicably funny, and I start to giggle.

"Your roommate has a girl in there?"

"He sure does."

"Lucky me." He doesn't sound happy. I wait for him to sigh, but he doesn't.

"Nope. Wrong! Lucky *him*!"

"Well, I guess you're gonna have to come home with me." I wish he sounded more enthusiastic. "No barfing out the window of my car tonight." On a positive note, he doesn't sound as mad as I expected; he's probably resigned to saving my ass for the fourth or the fifth—or is it the sixth?—time.

"YOU CAN SLEEP in my bed. I'll take the futon." Liam's bed is actually made up, all nice and neat and inviting. I wonder if he was hoping to get lucky tonight with some cute girl like tiny red-haired Dacia, and instead, all he got is me.

"Nah...I'll take the futon. I actually *love* futons. You can call me 'Futon Jase.' I don't mind." I don't think my joke made sense, but I'm nervous, and if I can make Liam laugh, I'll know he doesn't hate me. Even though he probably should.

He leads me past the futon lying flat on the floor in the corner. "You're gonna sleep in my bed. If you feel sick"—he's giving me direct orders, so I pay attention—"you can use this trash barrel." He hoists me onto the bed and pulls off my sneakers. Then he proceeds to less than gently remove my T-shirt and jeans.

"Are we gonna fool around now, Liam?" Hopefulness rings out in my voice. "I want to...I want to so much..." Last time we fooled around had been odd, in that everything but the happy ending had seemed so unfamiliar because Liam is what anybody would call *all man*—a first for me. But it had also been strangely magical. *Unforgettable* is the best way to describe it. Unforgettable, even as I'd tried so hard all summer to push it from my mind...but it...or maybe *he*...refused to leave.

I want to worship my hero, as he deserves. I want to show him with my body the tangle of feelings inside me, because my emotions are all caught up like a fish in a net...and the more I struggle to escape them, the more they entrap me.

"No, Jason. We're not gonna *fool around*. You're gonna get into this bed and sleep off your buzz, and I'm gonna sleep alone on the futon. And in the morning, I'm gonna drive you back to school and you're gonna suffer all day with one hell of a hangover." Liam's voice is cold enough to give me goose bumps. He walks to the little kitchenette and pours a glass of water, which he carries it to me and presses into my hand. "Drink the entire glass. In the morning, you'll be glad you did."

I follow his directions and then glance at him for a sign of approval, but his face is stone—cold, heartless, pissed-off-at-Jase-for-being-the-world's-biggest-dickhead. "Thanks, Liam."

"Now do me a favor and go to sleep." Without a glance at my face, he turns and heads for the futon.

"Come back here and look at me!" Sometimes words just spill out of my mouth. Especially when I'm plastered.

"Go to sleep, Jason."

"No...not until I see your eyes."

I hear the sigh. Liam's frustrated because he wants something he can't have. *I wonder what it is.* He turns back toward the bed but doesn't step closer. "Why are you doing this to me?"

The expression in his eyes doesn't match the coldness of his voice. He seems injured. "I made your eyes all sad and hurt."

"What are you talking about?" Liam is trying to keep his distance.

"I'm sorry I didn't call you. I...I wanted to."

"No worries, Jase. It's okay, and all forgotten. It's over now."

He called me *Jase*, and the hard edge to his voice is already softer. I'm making progress. "I don't want you to forget about me. I don't want it to be over."

Another sigh, louder than the last one. "It has to be over. And it's for the best...for both of us."

"I disagree strongly." My remark makes him laugh, but I ignore it. "And I *think* I know what it is now..."

"I have no clue what you're talking about. You're drunk. But go ahead and tell me what *it* is if you must. And then we can both go to sleep."

I may be drunk off my ass, but I can tell that he's humoring me. Still, I explain. "*This* is what *it* is—I don't really know if I can feel this way about any other guy in the world. But there's just something about *you*, Liam."

He steps to the bed and stares down at me with those piercing dark eyes I've missed so much. "You're drunk, and you don't know what you're saying."

I yawn. "Okay, then. I guess I'll have to tell you the same thing again in the morning." I turn on my side. "Night, Liam."

I'M INCREDIBLY THANKFUL for the trash bucket beside the bed when I wake up in the morning. I lean to the side and make good use of it.

"You okay, man?" The question comes from across the room.

"Been better."

Liam makes this chuckling sound, as if he's enjoying my misery. "I'll get you something for your headache." From my spot on the bed, I can see him walk across the room to the bathroom. He brings me a bottle of Advil and then grabs my glass. "Let me fill this up for you. And when I do, I want you to drink it all."

It feels comfortable in my heart when he tells me what to do. Maybe because I know he's right in everything he suggests. Or maybe it's for reasons I'd rather not analyze. "Thank you, Liam." I seem to say this a lot.

"No problem." Liam hasn't yet put his T-shirt on, as he'd rushed to get the pain meds upon waking up. He's a tall guy, and rugged, too, but the overall effect isn't so much like a tank, but more like a grizzly bear. His chest is covered in a blanket of light-brown curls; his arms and legs, the same. Liam's the picture of masculinity, and I wouldn't want him to look any different. "Time for you to get up so I can take you back to your dorm. It's almost ten, so your roommate should be finished with his nocturnal activities by now."

I get that just-slapped feeling again, and I don't appreciate the sting. "Liam..."

He sits down on the edge of the bed. "Jason, there's no use trying to force something between us that isn't there."

I sit up and try to ignore a blinding rush of pain in my temples. "Who's forcing anything? I thought you liked me." I sound like a child.

Liam picks up my hand from my lap. "Of course, I *like* you. And I'll always *like* you. But I was getting carried away with...with my feelings for you. I took it too far."

"You took it only as far as I wanted it to go."

"You were emotionally unstable, and I think I took advantage of that."

"That's not what happened, and you know it."

We're staring at each other now, really staring, as if this will somehow help us figure things out. "Listen, Jason. There's a lot of shit that's happened in my life you don't know. Shit about me and my family...that might lead me to be... Forget it. I can't explain this to you."

"I think you just were. Keep talking."

"It comes down to this— Something in me wants to help you, and needs to protect you... See where I'm going with this?"

I shake my head. "No."

"You aren't sure if you're gay, and guess what? Neither am I—how's that? But there's just something about how I feel when I'm with you...about how it feels when I take care of you. You bring out certain instincts in me."

There's silence while we both digest what he said. After a minute passes, I say, "I think I told you this last night, but I'm going to say it again. I couldn't feel the way I do for anyone but you—male or female. And I feel so much...I think I could fall in love with you." I'm in shock that I revealed this truth because I haven't fully grasped it yet.

His eyes widen. "You didn't exactly say *that* last night."

"Well, everything is a little bit clearer this morning."

He starts rambling. "I was hurt when you didn't call. I let myself...I let myself worry about you and... I really cared for you...and then...you never returned my calls and..."

"Climb in bed?" I lift up the sheets and pat the spot beside me.

Liam glances up and to the left, as if he's assessing the benefits and drawbacks of joining me between his sheets. "I...uh...I don't know, man." But even as he says this, he does it...he climbs into the bed. We stretch out beside each other, our shoulders touching.

"Will you hold me?" I ask.

He doesn't answer in words but pulls me onto him and sighs.

I press my ear to his furry chest and listen for the sound I love. When I hear the steady pounding, I sigh, too. "How about we just *try* to be together? You know, we don't worry about whether we're gay or straight or bi or whatever."

"You think that's realistic?" He's skeptical—and maybe so am I—but this is my life, and I'm not going to live by rules I didn't make and don't want.

I learned that much from loving Ginny, who was everything I wasn't in the very best of ways, and I'm going to put the lesson to action in my life. It's the least I can do in honor of her memory.

"I think that I'm a human being and you're a human being, and if we want, we can be two human beings who fall in love. It's that simple." I'm again reminded of Ginny, but not in the usual gut-wrenching way. "Labels are for suckers" was the first thing she ever said to me. I think she knew what she was talking about.

Gay, straight, bi, pan...all labels, and I don't need them.

I really think we can live this way.

Liam allows the loudest sigh I've heard since I met him, and then he shrugs. "This isn't in any way simple, you know."

It really doesn't matter that what I'm proposing is complicated. But I do have something else I need to say. "And I'm sorry for what I did last summer. I was scared of the wrong thing—of being gay—of living a life I'd never before considered. Now I'm scared of the right thing—of losing you."

Liam is quiet for so long I wonder if he's fallen asleep or, worse, chosen to refuse my request that we give *us* a try. Finally, he takes in a deep breath and says very softly, "'Kay."

With Liam's utterance of that single syllable, that half a word, I have a boyfriend.

WHEN LIAM AND I get back to campus and he walks with me to RetroHouse, we don't hold hands. It doesn't seem like the natural thing to do, and I vowed, just this morning, in fact, that I'm not going to do what's expected of me, but rather what feels right.

BJ's overnight guest is just leaving as we arrive at my room. She smiles shyly but manages not to blush at all, and makes her exit, shoes dangling from her fingertips. BJ is glowing in a way that's new.

"Dacia's a cool girl...such a super cool girl." He stares after her as she walks to her room down the hall. "I might be in love."

I can relate. I don't say so, but I glance at Liam, and he's studying me. "This is Liam Norcross. The guy I told you about."

BJ snaps out of his love trance and throws himself into Liam's arms. "You. Are. The. Man."

Liam is at a loss for words.

"You saved my bro's ass, and I wanna thank you somehow. Like, wanna meet a whole slew of freshman girls who'll be thrilled to show you some major hero worship?"

Liam gently pushes BJ back and says, "Thanks, but no thanks."

"Get used to having Liam around. You're going to be seeing a lot of him." I'm not going to spell it out for BJ, but I'll give him lots of clues and plenty of fair warning.

"You guys are having like a total bromance!" BJ laughs so loudly it causes a return of my brain-splitting headache. "I gotta go get some food…used up a lot of energy last night." He makes an "I had sex" gesture. "You guys wanna come along?"

Liam shakes his head, and I say, "I think we're just going to hang out here for a while."

"Yeah, right…go ahead and chill. Sorry—not sorry—if our room smells like sex." And with that classy warning, he's off to the dining hall.

"I can't explain BJ. But I *can* apologize for him." I lead Liam into my room. "Welcome to my humble abode."

Liam glances around at our undecorated, slightly messy dorm room. "Cool."

"It's not even slightly cool." I perch on the edge of the bed and gesture for Liam to sit beside me. "Is the reason you decided not to live in RetroHouse because you didn't want to run into me?" I ask this bluntly, embracing the new, honest me.

"I'm gonna level with you, man. When you didn't call me back last summer, I got messed up in the head. And I figured that running into you every other day wouldn't help me get over you."

I touch his thigh. It's rock hard beneath his black jeans. "I'm sorry I screwed up your housing."

Liam shakes his head. "You know, I'm actually glad I have my own place off campus. I think I've had enough of dorm life." He again checks out the standard college guy mess that is our room. "Maybe you did me a favor."

I'm also happy we'll have a place away from school to hang around, so we won't feel like we're under a microscope. Students and faculty know we're two of the survivors of the shooting in the theater, and me sleeping in his dormitory room in RetroHouse would have created gossip we don't need to be subjected to. "I appreciate your place off campus, too. It feels more relaxing than here. A little more like a home."

Liam smiles— It's honest and open and terrifying and brilliant, and it warms me in places that have always been, at most, tepid.

BJ was right: Liam is the man.

Chapter Fourteen

WE'VE BEEN "TOGETHER" for a week now. It's ironic that the thing I worried about most— suddenly *being bisexual* when I'd never before thought of myself that way—is not what actually ends up bothering me. Being with a man: anybody would think this would be the sticking point when it comes to being romantically involved with another very masculine guy who's also never before thought of himself as anything but straight. But no, my problems are never that cut-and-dry.

The bigger problem is that I suspect Liam is holding something back from me. I'm aware I don't have the right to demand access to every personal detail of his life before I entered it, but whatever he's holding back is hurting him. And that hurts me. Which hurts *us*.

Tonight is the first night since the evening of my drunken display of brutal honesty that we're staying together—as in, sleeping together—at his place. By mutual agreement, we've allowed our new status as a couple to gradually sink in all week, during which time we've only met for dinner twice. Our conversations were stilted at best, probably because we were sitting in the crowded RetroHouse dining hall, being stared at from all sides. It's Friday night, Liam invited me to stay with him in his apartment, and I agreed. *Alone* is the only way we're going to truly learn about each other.

Liam is always quite chivalrous. He refuses to let me take public transportation to his apartment, insisting he come pick me up at my dorm. I'm secretly glad, as I'm still reluctant to put myself in small, enclosed spaces with people I don't know well, like a bus.

I slide into the passenger seat of his car and fight the urge to lean toward him for a kiss. We haven't yet reestablished our physical relationship; I'm hoping we'll find it this weekend. I want intimacy with him. Not just the sexual aspect of it, but the emotional bonding. He must want connection, too, as he reaches across the console and squeezes my hand. I cling to his wide palm.

As always, Liam looks impressive with a rough-and-tumble style that's unique. His blond spikes of hair are swept up and to one side, and he wears jeans, a baseball T-shirt, a black leather jacket, and thick-soled boots.

He mentioned in his last text message that he wanted to eat dinner somewhere off campus tonight, so I tried to appear neater than my usual basketball shorts and T-shirt. I'm wearing a button-down white oxford shirt and my least worn pair of jeans, and of course, my standard dress-up boat shoes. I shaved extra-close and spent way too much time fixing my dark waves just perfectly. I'm even wearing cologne.

Liam studies me for a moment but says nothing about how I look. "You ready to go?"

I toss my pack in the back seat. "Any time you are."

And just like that, we're off.

"You into Thai food? Or are you more a steak guy?" I glance at his profile as he drives. I like what I see, but I'm not sure whether I should tell him, so I don't.

"I guess I'd prefer steak. I never know what to order at Thai restaurants."

"Then steak it is."

Within a few minutes, we're downtown, and he's parking outside Charlie's Steakhouse. I climb out of the car before he can come around to help me, which seems to frustrate him. He shakes his head and reaches out to close my door.

Our roles in this relationship are in question. Both of us are doing the best we can to be "the man" in the relationship, which makes no sense because we're both men. Inside the front door of the restaurant, a pretty hostess who I recognize from my photography class greets us. She peers from one of us to the other, as if she isn't sure which flavor of eye candy she prefers—rugged, husky, hairy, and blond or sleek, smooth, slim, and dark.

"Know of any parties tonight, guys?" She winks as she seats us in a corner booth. She obviously thinks we're loading up on food prior to a night of partying, when we're actually on our very first official date. "Maybe we can meet up somewhere when I get off work."

Liam is gentle in his discouragement. "It's not a party kind of night for us. But there's always something going on at RetroHouse."

The hostess appears puzzled, unused to rejection, but she smiles and thanks him. After another long stare at me, she strides back to the hostess table. Meanwhile, I struggle to accept that I've voluntarily placed myself in an enclosed space with a bunch of strangers who have not been frisked for weapons.

As soon as we're seated, Liam hooks his ankle around mine. I suck in a quick breath, which I think he hears.

"This okay with you?"

"It's actually...really good." I want to get to the heart of the matter that's weighing on me before we order dinner. "Something's been on my mind."

"Yeah, what?" Liam gazes at me from across the table, and it hits me that I've made the right choice in throwing *most* of my caution to the wind and becoming involved with him. His eyes are breathtaking—the most intelligent and compassionate eyes I've ever seen—and I want him to always look at me this way. There's also concern in his expression; he's worried about what I'm going to ask.

"Last weekend, you started to tell me there were things about you I don't know. And I'm starting to believe these things are hurting you."

Liam's stunning gaze drops to his lap.

"I want you to trust me with the stuff in your past that hurts."

"Shit." He doesn't glance up. He slides a few inches to the outer edge of the booth as if contemplating escape.

"We don't have to talk about it if you don't want to, but I can help you cope with your problem, whatever it is."

He replies too quickly. "Okay...so it's like this... I still feel like shit because I let my buddies die in that theater...it's not easy for me to live with." He grits his teeth and swallows hard before he looks at me again. There's more behind the haunted expression than I'd realized. "And...I lost somebody else a long time ago...in a fire. Not a subject I'm much into discussing. But there it is...and it still gets to me every now and then. Not gonna lie."

A fire. He lost "somebody" in a fire. I want to know who, when, how...all of it. But I have a feeling he just confided more in me than he's ever confided in anyone else, so I don't press him for details. "Thanks for telling me that."

Liam reaches across the table and takes my hand in his. A public first for us, and I wait for my own reaction to it— embarrassment, shame, worry? I experience none of these; all I feel is relieved I'm the one sitting across from him, listening to a tiny measure of his pain, and holding his hand. "Yeah, sure. No worries."

Sometimes when he says no worries, I think it's code for *you might want to worry about this, dude.*

"So how about we check out the menu?"

"Sounds like a plan."

DINNER IS GREAT and not nearly as awkward as sitting together in the school cafeteria being analyzed by the masses. Liam takes the long route home, and I'm not sure whether this is a stalling tactic or just a relaxing, scenic ride through the rolling hills of our Vermont college town. At his apartment, he parks, grabs my bag, and escorts me to the door. Standing in front of his apartment, he says very softly, "This...uh...tonight means a lot to me."

I hope he means we're going to find our way back to each other tonight. In every way.

Once we're inside, he grabs a bottle of wine, and we sit on his futon, which is now folded up into a couch. He makes no move to put on the television or music—instead pouring the wine—and I don't miss the background noise at all. I'm hoping to soon hear the thudding of his heart.

"It's not so weird as I thought...you know, being out in public...on a date with you...another guy." Someone had to say it.

Liam looks at me, tilts his head, and smiles. "We aren't exactly out of our own little closet yet."

"You know, I've faced death twice. I lost the person who was closest to me to a brutal act of violence. I don't care what the people on the other side of the closet door think."

"Same here." I've barely sipped the wine, but he takes my glass, places it on the low coffee table beside his, and leads me to the bed. "But the truth is, Jase, I never have."

This is an area where we're different, and it's one of the things about Liam that reminds me of Ginny. Neither cares what the crowd is thinking or doing.

No words are spoken as we stare at the bed, but I'm not troubled by the silence. I've shared some of the most significant moments in my life with Liam, and he's about to express to me how much he cares. And I'm going to show him how mutual that sentiment is. There really are no perfect words for this moment, so silence is better.

Before we lie down, we sit together on the edge of the bed. The kiss he places on my lips would be the subject of poetry if I were a flowery lyricist. But with proper motivation such as this, I might be inspired to give poetry another try.

After the spectacular kiss, his fingers are on the buttons of my shirt; he never shifts his gaze from my eyes as he unbuttons each one. He pushes it off my shoulders, pulls my T-shirt over my head with a swift stroke, and studies me. I know what he's thinking, as it shows in his wider-than-usual eyes. He's thinking he's never seen anything as beautiful in the world as my naked chest, and he's remembering how close he came to losing me, on more than one occasion, for more than one reason. His touch, a feather-light caress I had no idea he was capable of, shoots tremors of desire into my core.

I want to take off his T-shirt, but my motivation is different with Liam than it was with Ginny. I need to run my fingers through the thick curls on his chest, to lose myself in his strength and masculinity. He rips his shirt over his head. The deed is done without my assistance, and I'm surprisingly fine with my lack of participation.

What happens next results from pure instinct. Before we have a chance to explore with our hands, we spontaneously clutch each other and pull our bare chests together, joining our bodies in a way that isn't so much sexual as it is spiritual. When we finally release each other, our pants and boxers come off in a heated rush. I don't think any buttons or zippers were undone in the process. Everything was just yanked off and dropped to the floor.

I'm the first to reach out and touch. Although I like it when Liam takes charge, as he did that night last summer, it needs to be this way tonight. I need to initiate the intimacy, to prove that this is truly what I want.

I wrap my fingers around his swollen dick, and Liam groans deeply, which breaks the spell of silence. He returns the gesture, reaching out to hold my dick, which is as ready for action as his. Here we sit, our hands and eyes on each other, and I can't deny it's very different from anything else I've experienced, even from the single night we were intimate last summer. Sometimes, *different* is also *better*.

"I wanna make love to you tonight, Jase. Can I?" His voice doesn't break on the words. I couldn't have asked with such confidence.

I nod and then gift him with verbal willingness. "Yes, want to make love too."

"Tell me what you want...me to do." He sighs. I think he means *who's gonna do what to who?*

I answer with honesty. "I want you to fill me." *Isn't being on the receiving end of penetrative sex the ultimate in hero worship?* I'll be giving myself to him, and it's what I want. His close-lipped smile indicates he hoped this would be my preference.

"Jase..." He whispers into my ear, and chills rush over every inch of my chest. "You know I haven't ever been with a man?"

"You'll know what to do." I don't whisper. Instead, I speak softly, as I want to relay my confidence with the tone of my voice.

"You're right…I'll know." He smiles again, and this time, it's more deliberate, and I believe him. And I feel certain I love him. A long list of logical reasons for my sudden passion doesn't come rushing into my mind; it's more of a deep-seated inner knowledge.

Liam seems motivated and gets right to business. He leans to his bedside table and pulls from the top drawer the things we'll need. I'm glad he's prepared. Without a word, he pushes me onto my stomach and squirts something cool and moist on his fingers, which he applies to my ass without expertise, but he makes up for it with thoroughness. I feel a lot like a sixteen-year-old virgin as Liam's unwieldy fingers massage and then enter me. It's incredibly intimate to be touched this way. I blurt out, "I think I might come."

"Me too," he says, and in the middle of this clumsy and intimate moment, we're able to stare into each other's eyes and laugh. That we can do this is a positive sign, or more likely, a gift. Liam clears his throat and utters, "Let's slow down…there's no hurry tonight. And when I come, I want it to be inside you."

Chills spread through my groin. "Words like those are not going to help me to slow down, Liam." We laugh again.

Liam takes control in the same way he did last summer. He explores me thoroughly with eager fingers until I can tolerate the new sensation without too much squirming. Eventually, the probing eases, and Liam lies on his stomach beside me, and we again start to kiss. He breaks away from me after every third or so kiss, to study my expression, to kiss my eyes, to watch my face as he inserts a single finger, or two, more deeply.

"I want you more than you'd ever believe," he confesses.

"I'm ready…I'm r-ready for you now." My voice is shaky, but he gets the message and nods.

I assume he's going to climb onto my back to enter me from behind, because it fulfills my mental image of two men making love, but he doesn't. He could be afraid the position will bring me back to the worst of days, when he climbed on my back to push me under the seats in the theater in order to save my life. Gently, Liam presses on my side, and I roll again onto my back. "I want to look into your eyes." He kneels and lifts my ass onto his thigh and quickly pulls a condom on. Without a word, he raises my left leg to his strong shoulder and guides himself inside me, his expression tense with need and concentration.

My body tries to fight the pressure of invasion. But Liam's gentle persistence is greater than my body's resistance, and once he pushes inside me to a certain point, the struggle ends. His need has won this brief but intense battle, and he slides fully inside me.

"Oh, God...you're in me..." The cry comes from my gut—not the most intelligent of observations—but it seems to move him.

Liam's eyes are wet, but it's with the intensity of pleasure, not sadness. "Yeah...please say it's good for you."

I'm awed by the full, stretched sensation, but I'm not sure "good" is the right word for it. Before I respond, I take my dick in hand and begin to stroke. With the unique dual sensation of Liam deep inside me and friction where it counts, I'm able to say honestly, "Move in me...and it will feel better than good."

He struggles to keep his eyes open. "I need to go fast..." His words come in a rush.

"I do too." He immediately quickens his pace, and I try to pump myself to match his thrusts, but soon any rhythm we'd established disappears. The result would best be called a frenzy of movement.

When I start to come, he stiffens, squeezes his eyes shut, and lets go as well. My release seems to last longer than ever before; there's time enough for its magic to leave a lasting imprint on my brain.

Liam's breathing doesn't slow down immediately. Instead, he sucks in a quick breath, swallows deeply, and says, "I'm going to tell you something...that maybe I shouldn't." I have no idea how he can talk at a time like this—whatever he's compelled to say must be important. "I'm gonna tell you...I just...I love you, Jase."

I haven't cried since last summer. I've wanted to, plenty of times, like when I got back to school and was missing Ginny because she should be here and not in a grave. And I wanted to cry when I thought I'd lost Liam for good. But I always held back my tears. Right now, I let go and cry out the depth of my passion for this man. "I wanted...to tell you I love you too...so much...but I was afraid..."

"No more fear." These are Liam's last words to me before he falls asleep.

Time to live life fully because you never know when it's all going to be over.

The most unique and meaningful and maybe even awkward experience so far in my life concludes the way it started, with an adoring kiss worthy of inspiring lyrical verse. I guess now I'm a poet.

Chapter Fifteen

I GLANCE DOWN at his head resting on my lap. He's asleep, and I should wake him as he's in the middle of studying for an Information Systems quiz that he wants to ace. But he seems so peaceful, and when he's sleeping, I can't see the haunted look in his eyes. It hurts so much to look at; I hate the thought of Liam being in any pain. But worse is the awareness that he's withholding something important from me. And maybe I haven't known him all that long, but it's clear he needs to come to terms with whatever is bothering him. So instead of waking him up, I reach down and push back his blond hair that is surprisingly silky, the way a child's hair might feel.

Liam and I have tumbled more easily and naturally into coupleship than I'd anticipated. Last summer, when I realized I'd developed intense feelings for him, I avoided him completely because I couldn't imagine how two "straight" guys could function effectively as boyfriends. I thought a romantic relationship would be impossible and trying to establish it could be torturous. *Maybe my need for him has nothing to do with romantic love,* I'd decided at the end of July, *and if I leave it alone, the need will go away.*

First of all, there's the issue of sex. This topic is of primary concern to most young men. I've always appreciated the way girls looked, smelled, sounded, and tasted. And it might be true I've never gone for soft, sweet ones, but nobody would ever question their femininity. I had a few girlfriends in high school, Carrie Dodd being the one I dated the longest. She was known as the prettiest in town but was also as tough as the fake nails she wore. It was part of her allure. I made a major effort to think of her as challenging and free-spirited, but eventually, I had to admit she was obstinate and narcissistic.

Then there was my college love, Ginny, who prided herself on being edgy and unconventional. Ginny was attractive in an alternative sort of way. Although her folks were quite well-off, she wore beat-up old clothes found at thrift shops and sported long ratty dreadlocks. The skin on her hands and legs was riddled with bumps and bruises from her favorite pastime, rock climbing, as well as scars from frequent falls from her mountain bike. And she was cynical, even distrusting, of certain aspects of society, which intrigued me beyond belief. I was fascinated by her complex mind; I wanted to learn from her. I'd even say I admired her. And we had great sex, even if I wasn't completely transparent with her about all of my innermost desires. Before I met Liam, though, I really hadn't been fully aware of what I wanted most in bed.

Liam hasn't told me much about his past relationships, other than he'd taken two different girls to the junior and senior high school proms, and spent a lot of time with a girl he'd met at a summer job painting houses, when he wasn't working at his best friend's family restaurant. He said he'd mainly participated in "physical relationships" with women, which I understood to be no-strings-attached hookups. From the very casual way he mentioned the ladies in his life, it seemed to me romance hadn't ever been his top priority. And he'd never considered the possibility he could be bisexual until he met me.

Sex hasn't turned out to be a problem for us. I always figured sexual desire was based on how sexy my partner appeared, but it isn't that way with Liam—not that Liam doesn't look good, because I think he's about as good-looking as a *guy* can be. But it's his protectiveness, gentleness, and devotion to me that takes me to a place where I'm moved to feel sexual desire. I wouldn't have believed this was possible had I not experienced it firsthand.

I think of making love to Liam as worshipping my hero. I want to see the tender expression on his face when he gets turned on, and I want to see the awe when I touch him, and he can't believe it feels so good.

I'm drawn to his inner strength. I can't deny that the romance started with the violence we survived together—that he rescued me from. I bonded easily with his heart and mind and soul; from there, bonding with his body wasn't a huge leap. I can't afford to lose what I've found with him.

His forehead wrinkles in his sleep, and I wonder what he's dreaming about. This brings to mind another aspect of a relationship with a guy that's challenging. In my relationships with girls, they never failed to stand up and scream when I did something stupid, and they chased after me if I tried to run away. But open communication is hard for Liam and me; we often hold back our thoughts.

I brush my fingers along the length of his long beard and linger on the bottom where it's squared off bluntly. "Hey, Liam, you have to wake up. You need to study." His dark eyes flutter open, and I'm lucky enough to witness an expression of pleasure at seeing my face. I feel warm, and it quickly turns into arousal, proving my theory that the love I see in his eyes leads me to desire.

"Sorry, I fell asleep."

"No apology necessary. You seem peaceful when you sleep, so it was all good."

Liam smiles and stifles a yawn. "I feel peaceful, Jase. You make me feel peaceful."

I want to plead with him to tell me what's bothering him, but I don't. He'll either clam up or give me a vague answer that will frustrate me. "Let's go to the dining hall and then the library. We'll study better on full stomachs."

"'Kay. I'm gonna go rinse off my face. Be back in a few." He pulls himself off the bed and rises to his full height. "You look sexy, sitting there with your book open. Just saying." He gazes at me for a minute, wearing a sweet smile, but that strange haunted expression clouds his eyes before he leaves the room.

I need to know what's causing his pain. Part of loving this hero of mine requires that I dive headfirst into the darkest parts of his mind so I can lift him into the light. I have an idea of how to figure out what puts the shadows in his eyes, but I'm reluctant to put it into action.

Chapter Sixteen

WORD IS OUT around school that something more is going on between Liam Norcross and Jason Tripp than just being survivors of the most violent event in the history of Batcheldor College. We've kept our relationship quiet for a month now, but it's hard to hide *inseparable*. Neither of us is dating women, and I'm missing in action all weekend, every weekend, because I stay at Liam's apartment. Students realize this is way beyond we-survived-hell-together behavior.

Maybe they think it's a "Post Traumatic Stress Romance," or hero worship to the nth degree. And maybe it *is* both of these things, or maybe it started that way but has evolved into more.

BJ was the first to figure it out, which really isn't surprising. Of the time Liam and I spend together on campus, much of it is in our dorm room—Liam and I sitting shoulder to shoulder on my bed, and BJ on the other bed, trying to figure us out. Like right now.

"So, do you guys feel as if you're totally over the Harrison Theater shooting? I mean, you act normal enough...in most ways."

Liam, sitting on my bed and leaning against the wall, looks to me to provide an answer. I shake my head and say, "I'm not over it. I don't think I'm ever going to be over it. Whenever I'm out in public, I'm aware of the risk."

"And we both question our actions in the theater last April, every day," Liam adds, still watching me closely.

"Yeah, we both have a ton of guilt...mine's about Ginny." The most difficult part of living through that night is the survivor's guilt. "I don't think I did all I could have to help her." I'm proud that I'm able to voice this thought aloud; I've been struggling with the guilt for months.

"You're a journalism major, Jase. You should write about all the shit that went down that night, and also what happened when DeSalles came after you guys at the hotel...you know, so other people can relate better. And then some Hollywood dude can make it into a movie."

BJ's suggestion is a good one because a lot of Ginny and my friends stare at Liam and me rather scornfully, as if I'm somehow cheating on Ginny's memory. But I'm not ready to write about it yet; I'm still making sense of the experience. And I don't think I'll ever be ready for the movie version of that night.

"Maybe I'll write about it someday."

Liam reaches out and squeezes my knee. He's doing what he does best: making sure I'm okay.

"So, I'm just gonna put it out there... Jase, you were straight last year, and you're pretty much gay now. Did the trauma turn you guys gay?"

Liam stiffens. I worry he'll come back at BJ with a "fuck you" or worse. I cover his hand with mine to calm him, which is what *he* often does for me. BJ isn't cruel; he's just inappropriately direct and a little bit nosy. And his question is a good one. In fact, Liam and I have asked ourselves the very same thing. "What happened at the theater bonded us in a way we can't reverse," I explain.

"We don't want to reverse it." Liam's gaze hasn't strayed from my face. It's unusually penetrating as this is a subject we don't fully understand.

"So you two just fell hard—and you both being dudes wasn't a factor, right? I kinda get it. See, I was nuts about Ezra Koenig of the indie band, Vampire Weekend, for my entire senior year of high school. In my eyes, the guy could do no wrong." He lowers his voice to a conspiratorial tone. "I wouldn't have kicked him outta my bed, no joke."

I don't know if BJ really gets it at all, but I nod. "Yeah, it's something like that."

"And I fell hard for Dacia and... *Shit!* I'm supposed to meet her at the student lounge in five minutes. We're gonna have coffee... You guys wanna join us? It'll be a double date!"

I blush at his suggestion, but Liam replies with a very straight face, "Yeah...a double date. Sounds good." And he's off the bed, tucking in his shirt in a split second. I think he's ready to go public with our relationship at school. It's going to be harder for me because all my friends knew about my relationship with Ginny; they're going to have plenty of questions about my sexual orientation.

And I have no concrete answers for them. I love Liam. It's that simple, and at the same time, it's completely confounding. I'm *in love* with him, too—with his strength and humor, his devotion, the way he comforts and saves me. The way he wouldn't and couldn't leave me—in the theater, when his life was at risk, or now. And this unique and powerful love leads me to want him in every way possible. I want him to see only me, and I want him to desire what he sees. I want to turn him on until he can't stand it any longer, and then I want to satisfy him. Our genders, our orientations, *must* take a back seat to these things. And so we embrace our at-first awkward, but not reluctant, bisexuality.

"I guess it's a coffee date, then." I jump off the bed and run my hands through my short hair to put it back into place. "But can I still have hot cocoa?"

Time to go public with this thing.

Chapter Seventeen

USUALLY, LIAM AND I don't watch the news— there's too much on it that brings out the haunted expression in his eyes, and most of it thoroughly depresses me. But since we're eating breakfast in a diner where there's a television mounted on the wall above the bar, we're half listening to the day's events between bites of pancakes and conversation. We can't miss the report that a disgruntled employee intentionally set a fire at an Imax theater where a group of school kids was on a class field trip. One student had been killed. This piece of news hits us where it hurts most: murder in a theater and death by fire.

The troubled look I see every so often—a darkening of his eyes, a lowering of his eyebrows, a hollow expression— appears on Liam's face and refuses to leave. As he drives me back to RetroHouse, he remains preoccupied.

After he parks, he reaches over the seat for my backpack, and I tug his sleeve lightly with my fingertips. He's so wrapped up in his dark thoughts that my touch startles him. He jolts as if I slapped him.

"Liam, you need to tell me what happened to upset you so much. Do you think I'm completely out to lunch? It's obvious the fire in the theater we saw on television reminded you of what happened in your past...so just *tell me* about it. We can talk it over." I grab his arm. "You'll feel relieved."

In an instant, Liam's face is bright red and practically steaming. I've never seen him so angry. He yanks his arm out of my grasp. "You have no fucking clue what you're talking about." It's as if he is staring right through me. "Take your bag." He shoves my backpack at me. "I'm gonna trust that you can walk safely back to the dorm on your own." Liam puts the car in drive and stares out the windshield as he waits for me to get out of the car.

I place my hand on his forearm. "Liam…"

Again, he shakes off my hand. "Just go."

THE NIGHT DRAGS on forever. I'm angry at how Liam snapped at me so unreasonably, and I'm devastated he refuses to confide in me. And I'm worried about him. The man who kicked me out of his car is not the one who so patiently walks by my side every day. I check my phone before I go to bed and there's a text message from him.

Liam: *Are you ok? Did you get back to your room w/out a problem?*

After the rush of relief that Liam still cares, a wave of confusion nearly knocks me over. I don't know how to reply.

Liam: *Jase, I'm sorry. Please forgive me for how I treated you.*

The anxiety that has built up during the past few hours clouds my mind. I can't find words to express how I feel.

Liam: *Please, Jase, text me one word just to let me know you're ok. I'm a mess.*

I have no interest in further torturing Liam, seeing as he's doing a damned good job without my help.

Jase: *I'm okay. It'll be okay.*

Within a few seconds of sending my message, I receive a final text.

Liam: *Thank you. I love you.*

I'm going to do something about this situation in the morning.

Chapter Eighteen

I SKIP MY first class to do research privately in my dorm room. I wait until BJ leaves, as there's something very wrong with the prospect of snooping into Liam's life while BJ prattles on and on about the wonders of Dacia's perfectly round ass.

The truth of the matter is, I could have done this search weeks ago, a month ago even, when I learned Liam had lost someone he cared about in a fire. But I didn't because I wanted Liam to come to me of his own free will and confide what's been disturbing him so much. It's become crystal clear he's not going to do this, and his inability to face his past is causing him, and us, pain. So I type the words in the search box: *Liam Norcross* and *fatal fire*.

The screen fills with links before I have time to blink. I click on the first one.

The Maine Fire Marshall's Office has identified the person killed in an early morning fire yesterday in Lockwood. Lucy Norcross, 12, was found in a second-floor bedroom of her family's home on Willow Street. The fire was called in at 3 AM on January 24. Faulty wiring was reportedly the cause.

I type in *Lucy Norcross obituary.*

> On January 24, 2008, Lucy Caroline Norcross, age 12, died in a tragic fire in her home. Lucy was the beloved daughter of David and Donna Norcross of Lockwood, Maine. She is survived by her older brother, Liam, age 14. Her funeral service will be held on Tuesday, January 29, at 2 PM at First Presbyterian Church on Broad Street, followed by a reception at The Williamsport Yacht Club. Lucy's family requests that in lieu of flowers, donations are sent to The Museum of Science in Boston, Massachusetts.

Liam lost his little sister in a house fire. This explains a lot, but questions flood my brain. *Was Liam in the house at the time of the fire? Does he blame himself for his sister's death? Could he hear her cries for help? How did his parents react to this loss?*

I can't know the answers to these questions without asking, which hasn't worked very well thus far. In fact, asking questions had just added stress to our fledgling relationship. But if I could meet Liam's parents, it would provide me the opportunity to get closer to the heart of the matter. I realize I've just figured out my next goal in helping Liam face his demons and hopefully put them to rest.

WE'RE SITTING IN the dining hall at lunchtime, after having kissed and made up in the hallway where we always meet at noon.

"Don't you think it's time we met each other's families?" I realize this request involves Liam meeting my opinionated mother, but I'm willing to make this sacrifice if it means getting a closer look at Liam's past.

"You don't wanna meet my folks." He seems very certain of this.

"Why not?"

He shifts on the bench. "They aren't too much into me and my life. You know, they're really busy."

"You think they'll be upset that you're bringing home a guy, not a girl?"

His smile isn't a happy one. "I don't think it will have much of an effect on them, one way or the other."

"Well, then, let's set it up. I really want to meet them. How far do you live from school?"

"About two-and-a-half hours." He tilts his head, clearly thinking. "And...does this mean I'm going to meet your parents, too?"

"If you want to, be my guest. But it's only just my mother. Dad is more or less a big no-show in my life."

Liam's expression is blank, as if he's uncertain what he's gotten himself into. He mumbles, "Both of my parents are no-shows in my life."

I act as if I don't hear his last remark because I'm focused on seeing his mom and dad for myself. "How about we do it this weekend? We can meet my mother on Saturday and your parents on Sunday."

He nods, rubs his beard, and replies, "Eat your lunch."

Chapter Nineteen

THIS IS GOING to be a complete disaster. I should have warned her that the "special person" I'm bringing home is a man. A very manly man. And I should have warned *him* that mine is not your average mother.

Shit.

But I have a reason for doing this, and it will be worthwhile in the end.

Keep on telling yourself that, Jason. Maybe you'll start to believe it.

We pull up in front of the house, a tiny, seen-better-days chocolate-brown ranch in a neighborhood where the developer went bankrupt well before his dream of turning a thick patch of pine forest into "affordable, yet stylish, housing for frugal NH families" was complete.

I'm not sure who decided that low-budget, vinyl-sided ranches are stylish, but growing up among the unfinished foundations of ten more of them hadn't been bad at all. My friends from the other frugal families in the unfinished neighborhood and I played in and around the houseless basements, pretending we were living in a village on Mars. Great food for the imagination, but ultimately, Mom forbade me from playing on the abandoned foundations, as "knees skinned on rough concrete don't heal neatly."

Liam pulls his car into our patched-up driveway, and I glance at him to see how harshly he's judging his surroundings.

"I do what I can with the exterior, but it's like applying lipstick to a pig." My voice is oddly high-pitched. When I last went home for a visit at the end of September, I mowed the lawn and trimmed the shrubs to appear as respectable as possible. My meager efforts didn't amount to much, I realize as I stare at my home-sweet-home.

"It's fine, Jason. No worries." Code for: time to worry. Liam looks as if he's about to be dragged, naked and squealing, across the roughly poured cement foundation next door.

"It'll be fun. You'll see." The tone of my voice is not convincing.

I know it's bad when Liam quotes Lola from the Beachcomber Bar and Grill. "Guess I'm feeling kinda like a puke stain on the white-collared button-down shirt of life."

I can't help but laugh. "Mom is going to love you." My sweet sentiment sounds more like a question than the affirming statement it was meant to be. Time to let whatever will be, be.

Liam snorts, and we get out of the car that my mother will no doubt refer to as a death trap. He follows me up the untidy walkway, only stumbling once on that damn brick that has stuck up too high since I did my best to replace a crumbled one in seventh grade.

I smell double-chocolate fudge brownies the instant Mom opens the door. "Jason, dear, you made it home, and you're only thirty minutes late this time—how considerate!" She glances past me to Liam, and her mouth forms the pucker of someone who's been dared to suck an extra-juicy lemon. She points at Liam. "*That* is the 'special person' you told me about?" Yes, complete with air quotes.

Our visit has started out precisely as I anticipated— miserably—so I know things can go nowhere from here but up. "Mom, I'd like you to meet Liam Norcross...my, uh...my boyfriend."

Thankfully, Liam is right there to catch Mom when she falls into an apparent faint. Saving people's asses is my boyfriend's specialty.

Five minutes later, we're seated at the kitchen table, Mom fanning her face and neck with the current Vogue magazine and Liam stuffing Mom's famous double-chocolate fudge brownies into his mouth like the cocoa bean tree is an endangered species. "These are fantastic, Mrs. Tripp. Did I hear you right when you said that this is *your own* secret recipe?"

Neither Ginny nor Carrie would take so much as a single bite of Mom's pride and joy brownies. Carrie was compelled to watch her perfect waistline, and Ginny didn't much care for chocolate and refused to humor my mother by indulging in a brownie and faking a chocolate orgasm. Needless to say, Mom is basking in the glow of the "you are the Brownie Top Chef" compliments that Liam is lavishing on her, and I can tell she's warming up to him.

"So Liam, you're from Maine?"

He stops chewing only long enough to say, "Yes, ma'am, I'm from Lockwood to be exact."

"Oh, that's a quaint little town, so close to the ocean."

Liam's face clouds over, but he agrees. "Yes, it's nice there."

"And you're studying business? A very practical choice. Jason insists upon studying journalism. Knowing him, he probably wants to travel to some third world country to report on the miseries of the local population's lives, and in the process, he'll catch some contagious disease like Ebola and...oh, dear..."

"Mom, I'm probably going to end up working for a small-town newspaper reporting about something like the new playground equipment at the local elementary school."

"That may very well be true, but grade school kids are notorious carriers of ringworm, so my suggestion is that you wash your hands frequently."

I'm so frustrated at her dramatics I want to reach out, grab Mom by the shoulders, and shake some sense into the woman.

"Good one, Mrs. Tripp! You're such a riot!" Liam actually thinks she's joking. *That* makes me want to laugh, but what's even more humorous is my mother's reaction to his incorrect interpretation.

"Oh...oh, yes. I can be quite a card under the right circumstances." She bats her eyelashes in his direction, and I again resist the urge to throttle her.

As soon as my mother, the card, has a chance, though, she drags me out of the kitchen and into our tiny pantry. "Why did you not tell me you were gay, Jason? Did you really think I would cast you out on the street where you'd most certainly get lice and walking pneumonia, simply because you're a homosexual?"

"Mom...it's not like that. It's just that Liam and I—"

"I have one word of advice for you, seeing as you're a gay man."

I have no choice but to wait for it.

"Condoms."

My cheeks start to burn in a way that can only happen when your mother advises you to use condoms with your new male lover.

"And frankly, I'm relieved that you chose a man like Liam. Your taste in girls was atrocious. That Ginny was so standoffish—I hate to speak ill of the dead, but I'm going to level with you—she was the most difficult girl I've ever met."

Well, this is news to me. "Mom, Ginny wasn't difficult; she was just very direct...and aggressive, at times...and she refused to bow down to anyone."

Mom gives me a look that clearly implies, *isn't that what I just said—difficult?*

I sigh. "Whatever."

"Don't 'whatever' me, young man. Now, get back in there to your handsome boyfriend, and I'll make him some lemonade...and I'm going to use the *good* glasses."

Although she doesn't seem to be aware of the existence of bisexuality—and I don't make even the slightest attempt to explain it to her, as it may prove to be more frustrating than fruitful—I actually enjoy Mom a lot more in Liam's company than when she and I are alone. He diffuses her bossiness—largely because he doesn't fully understand her intention—and just laughs at her crazy remarks. At the end of our visit, she hugs and kisses him on his way out the door. Before she hugs and kisses me.

"And young man..." Mom calls across the driveway to Liam as we get into the car. "That vehicle you're driving is nothing but a death trap. I implore you to not exceed the highway speed of fifty-five miles per hour. Our sweet Jason's life is in your hands."

Liam drives very slowly all the way back to his apartment.

"I DON'T THINK we should waste our time going to my house today." Liam had a hard time sleeping last night, and his eyes, which in his case are truly the windows to his thoughts and moods, are bleary and dull this morning. "I can think of many other ways I'd rather spend a rainy afternoon." He looks at me and waggles his eyebrows. I don't bite.

"Eyes on the road, mister," I shoot him down with a smile. The sky is as dreary and gray as Liam's expression—it had rained, even poured, off and on, as we lay awake in bed waiting for the alarm on his phone to sound. "It's important that I meet your parents and see where you're from."

"This isn't even the same house I grew up in." He doesn't explain any further, I suspect because the house he grew up in burned to the ground when he was fourteen.

"Well, we don't have to stay all day. Let's just stop by for a quick hello and then head to the coast for a scenic drive. I haven't been out this way for ages. It really is beautiful."

A loud sigh accompanies an exaggerated eye roll. "Okay, since your every wish seems to be my command." He continues to drive, now wearing a scowl. I don't appreciate his tone, and it's actually quite unlike him to act so surly, but I'm still hopeful this trip to his hometown will be enlightening, and therefore worth it. I keep my thoughts about his bad attitude to myself.

My boyfriend is either extremely reluctant to arrive at our destination or he has taken my mother's "drive at a snail's pace when my son is in your car" suggestion to heart, as he cruises along at a maximum speed of thirty-five miles per hour. Still, I hold back on the criticism. It will get me nowhere faster than it would get me anywhere else.

We pull up in front of a modern home in a stately neighborhood that overlooks the rocky coastline of the Atlantic Ocean. It's the kind of street where, once a week, crews of eight men descend upon each home to mow the lawn and groom the shrubs and polish the exterior windows and vacuum the pool. The water view is dramatic but intimidating. And the gray sky only enhances the somber austerity of the huge pale-yellow house. It's beautiful, yet unwelcoming.

He parks his car on the smooth black driveway with a short screech. I swing open the door and get out. Liam exits the driver's side but makes no move to collect me or to wave at the occupants of his house or to really do much of anything except stand beside his car and brood. I'm feeling absolutely zero in the direction of warm and fuzzy here. He sends me a got-what-you-wanted glance, and says, "Come on, Jason."

I trail behind Liam as he makes his way to a side door in the third garage bay. He pulls out a key from his back pocket, unlocks it, and lets us in. We walk by a twenty-four foot, yellow Chaparral speedboat in the last garage bay, and then proceed past a shiny black Lincoln Navigator in the middle, and finally past a sleek silver metallic Jaguar XJ.

"Your dad has a lot of toys."

Liam shrugs. "They're Mom's toys, too."

We enter into an enormous sparkling kitchen—it's so clean I'd eat off the royal blue-and-white decorative tile floor without hesitation. The room sports black granite counters, oversized metallic appliances, and high ceilings. "You have *two* ovens and *two* refrigerators?"

"And two dishwashers." He isn't elbowing me and joking, so I know this is nothing more than Liam's way of life.

He told me once before that he was an only child, and I now know that to be sort of untrue. So I decide to see if I can get him to talk about it. I gesture toward the kitchen appliances. "All this for a family of three?"

Liam considers my question, and then replies in a dull tone, "My parents entertain a lot."

We stand here waiting for his parents to come to the kitchen to welcome us, but we wait for nothing. No one comes to say hello.

"You can sit in the living room. I'll go find my folks." He takes my hand and leads me to another oversized room, with a black leather sectional couch, several modern charcoal-gray suede chairs with matching ottomans, and a huge widescreen television. Just about everything else in the room is a shade of beige.

"Shit, Liam. Your television is more like a movie screen."

He glances at me. "It's just a TV, Jase." And then he heads for the stairs.

I should have predicted from his usual humble demeanor that the size of a television, the showiness of some vehicles, and the glamor of a house wouldn't mean a thing to Liam. In fact, he never mentioned to me that he lived in a multimillion-dollar mansion with a spectacular view of the Atlantic. I don't sit in the fancy chair or on the huge couch, but instead, I get started on doing what I'm here to do. I walk slowly around the enormous room, searching for something that will give me a clue as to the disaster Liam suffered in his youth. I come upon a small ivory-colored chest of drawers, neatly tucked behind the picture window's extravagant pale gold velvet curtains, and on it is a small framed photograph. The picture is of two children sitting cross-legged at the end of a dock, grinning at the person holding the camera.

Despite his toothless smile, I would know Liam anywhere; the expression in a person's eyes doesn't change over time. Though smiling, he's thoughtful—even uneasy— and appears very much aware of the tiny blonde girl beside him. The little girl is everything Liam is not; she is jovial and carefree and laughing through her broad grin. I assume this is Liam's little sister, Lucy.

The wooden frame displaying the photo of Liam and his sister is old, and its gray paint is chipped on the edges. It's probably the only item in the room that isn't shiny and new. I pick it up and flip it, and on the reverse side of the frame, *I love you, Lucy* is printed in purple marker, complete with two purple hearts, both of which say LN in the center.

After listening for the sound of voices on the stairs and hearing nothing, I continue my exploration of the grand living room. I walk to the huge fireplace that is built from piles of pale, flat, smooth stones. Above it is an enormous painting of the same little girl, but this image of her is in color. She's about ten years old, beautiful in an angelic way, and she's dressed in an old-fashioned ivory lace dress that makes her look like a child of the 1800s. Her smile is more demure than in the other photo, and there's a spark of high spirit in her eyes she just can't hide, although I think she might be trying. The frame, itself, is also a work of art. It's mostly white but has been painted golden yellow where the picture meets the frame, providing a sunburst effect. Across the top of the frame, in brilliant gold slanted script, is painted the name Lucy and across the bottom of the frame are the words, "The Light of Our Lives."

I find this statement to be rather heartless. *If Lucy is the light of their lives, what is Liam?* So as not to jump to an erroneous conclusion, I glance around the room in search of a comparable painting of Liam that boldly declares he is the other sun in their sky, but I find nothing. Aside from the painting of Lucy, the walls are all bare and white, with one small exception.

I step to the narrow wall beside the front door where there's a photograph of Liam in a cheap black document frame, the kind you can get at any pharmacy. Holding my breath, I lean in to examine it closely. It appears to be Liam's high school senior picture. The boy in the photo is the same Liam I know, but his face is thin and bare. He has no long squared-off beard and he isn't wearing the thick-framed black glasses that provide such an effective boundary between his dark eyes and the world. Liam's wearing a simple navy jacket and a traditional striped banker's-style tie, one that I'm pretty sure he wouldn't be caught dead in today. On the standard light-blue background to the left of his face, is a handwritten note. It's written in pencil, and is so tiny I need to squint to read it.

To Mom and Dad on my graduation day— I will make you proud.

Your son, Liam.

Although I haven't yet met his parents, this trip to Liam's home has already proved to be enlightening. *A picture tells a thousand words*. How very true. And these *three* pictures, the small snapshot of siblings on a dock in better days, the huge portrait of Lucy—the light of this family's life—and the plain commercial graduation photograph of Liam that marks his entrance into the adult world, with the pleading message begging his parents to notice him, tell much of the story.

I'm still staring at the modest photograph of Liam when he returns to the room. I turn around to see him with a woman—an obviously drunk woman.

She's tall and even-featured and blonde and appears as young as twenty-five, although I realize she must be twice that age. Dressed in crisp black jeans, a silky white blouse, black heels, and dripping in diamonds, she seems to fit perfectly into this formal setting. Without saying a word to greet me, she sits on one of the suede chairs.

"Mom, this is Jason Tripp. Jason, meet my mother, Donna."

The sound of ice jostling around in the bottom of a glass brings my attention to the small tumbler of amber liquid she grasps. I try not to stare at it, or compare her to my mother, who opened the door yesterday wearing an apron and an oven mitt, and I say, "I'm pleased to meet you, uh..." It wouldn't be appropriate to refer to her as Donna, so I go with her married name. "...Mrs. Norcross."

"Call me Donna. Donna, plain and simple." She doesn't appear very plain to me at all, and I find her strange remark disconcerting. I wait for her to look up and tell me how pleased she is to meet a close friend of her son's, but she doesn't seem to be aware of social decorum.

When it's clear she's not going to properly greet me, I step across the room to stand before her chair, carefully avoiding Liam's eyes because I know they'll express what he's thinking—*I told you we shouldn't have come here*—and I shake her hand. "It's nice to meet you, Donna. You have a beautiful home."

"Did you notice the portrait of our darling Lucy?" She struggles to rise from the chair, only succeeding with Liam's gentle assistance, and stumbles past me to the huge painting of her daughter. "Lucy was ten years old when she posed for this portrait. The artist said that she was the most beautiful child he had ever painted. And the sweetest too." Her voice is dreamy as she reminisces.

I sneak a glance at Liam. He's staring at the floor.

"We lost her when she was twelve." She sighs, long and loud, and it makes me think of Liam's frequent sighs. Then her voice lowers. "But...we still have Liam." She sniffs and spins around sharply, which surprises me because she isn't very steady on her feet. "And now our *son* Liam has a *friend.*" Donna grimaces, making no attempt to hide her disgust at our relationship.

"You *know* what he is to me...*who* he is to me." Liam steps up beside me protectively, but her words don't hurt me. Her bitter attitude toward her son, however, does.

"Ah, yes, Liam. But what's another disappointment for your father and me?"

The silence is extremely awkward. Liam breaks it by suggesting quietly that we leave. I'm about to take his hand when Donna calls out in an outdoor voice, "That's right, Liam. Run away. Just like you did *that night...*"

Liam and I gasp. "Come on, Jase...we're outta here." He grabs my wrist and pulls me toward the front door, but before we can open it, it swings into us, and a man bursts through, holding four takeout cups of coffee in a drink holder.

"Liam!" He places the tray of coffees on a desk near the door and reaches for a hug.

Liam embraces his father. "Dad, we were just leaving."

"Hey—I cut my golf game short to see you and your...your *boyfriend*, or whatever you wanna call him."

Liam glances at me with a question in his eyes, and I nod. "Okay, Dad, but we can stay for one cup of coffee."

"Well, good because that's all I brought! And your mother wouldn't know how to brew a pot of coffee to save her life."

Donna snorts and asks, "What do I want with coffee, David?"

"Think about what you just said, Donna."

She doesn't seem to pick up on the you-are-a-drunk-and-need-coffee-to-sober-up message and stares at him blankly.

"And remember, *you* said it, I didn't," Mr. Norcross snipes and turns to the desk to get a cup of coffee. "Help yourselves, boys."

Liam removes two cups of coffee from the desk and returns to me. He doesn't take a cup to his mother, who needs one more than the rest of us put together. "We might as well sit down." He's as wary as a cat in a bathtub.

Liam's father gestures toward the couch, where we sit. Donna drops into the same chair as before, but Mr. Norcross remains on his feet by the fireplace. "So, introduce me to...to this *fine young man* you have brought home to us." The man laughs as if he's joking, but I'm pretty sure he's not.

"This is Jason Tripp. Jason, you've kinda already met my father, David Norcross."

Again, I'm not greeted with the offer of a proper handshake, but this time I'm not surprised. I don't bother to get up.

"Where are you from, Jason?"

"I'm from Wilson, NH, sir."

"I know where that is... Shackville, USA, if I remember correctly...near the border of Vermont. Am I wrong?" He laughs again. "You sure know how to pick 'em, son."

Liam stands abruptly as if to confront his father, and a drop of black coffee from his paper cup drips onto the white carpet.

"Jesus Christ, Liam—you stop by for a visit and trash my house!" Donna is furious. She stands and staggers to the stairs. "I need a damned drink."

"Good job, Donna. Just go upstairs and leave me alone with the pansies...and you know I've never cared much for flower arrangements."

"That's it, we're out of here." Liam holds his hand out. I take it and rise. "And this, Jason, is just another day in the life at the Norcross house."

"Oh, poor baby! Your life is *so damned* tough, Liam." David Norcross sucks down the end of his coffee and crumples the cup. "I'm an investment banker, Jason." He stares into my eyes. "And a very successful one from what you can see." He gestures to the gorgeous living room. "My wife and son don't appreciate what I do for them...all the sacrifices I make to keep them living in this style."

I have no idea how to respond, but Liam starts tugging at my hand, and I know this visit has come to an end. I came here to find out more about Liam's pain, and I think I have a pretty decent picture of it now.

"But Lucy... All I had to do was look into her eyes, and I could tell we were on the same page in a way Donna and Liam never could be and never will." He rubs his eyes in a show of emotion, but I want to rub mine because I can't believe what I'm seeing—the most dysfunctional family in the humble state of Maine. Make that in all of New England.

For Liam alone, I dig deep and say, "Well, I'm glad to meet you, David. And thanks for the coffee."

"Yeah. Yeah, sure." He steps back to admire the life-sized portrait of his daughter.

Liam and I exit through the front door instead of heading back through the huge garage filled with toys. We actually *run* down the walkway to his car because neither of us can get away from the palpable misery in that pale-yellow house fast enough. Once we're inside his car and backing down the driveway, I ask, "Are they going to be furious at you now, because of the stuff you guys said to each other?"

Liam stops the car at the end of the driveway, studies me with a smirk, and then he shakes his head. "Nope. What you just witnessed is normal daily life at my house. I'd call it par for the course interaction. In fact, I think our little get-together with my folks went fairly well."

"Shit." It's the only thing I can think of to say, except for, "That sucks."

"Let me quote my father, if you don't mind." Liam throws the car in drive. "You said it, I didn't."

Chapter Twenty

WE GO STRAIGHT back to Liam's apartment as the Norcross family's offensive behavior pretty much killed any hopes we had for a romantic drive along the rocky coast of Maine. The return trip seems overly long, which is probably because Liam refuses to speak. I don't think he's angry at me; he's just consumed with worry and despair. I plan to discuss this entire situation with him tonight.

When we arrive at Liam's place, I suggest he take a hot shower while I make grilled cheese sandwiches and chicken noodle soup. He needs a few minutes by himself, and I need time to figure out how to begin the conversation that is essential to heal Liam's distress.

The color is back in his cheeks when he emerges from the shower, a thick, white towel wrapped around his waist.

"You sure know how to dress for dinner," I say, placing the bowls of soup beside the sandwiches on his tiny kitchen table in the corner.

"I didn't think you'd mind," Liam replies.

"You were right... I don't. You must be starving."

He drops into a chair and stares at me across the table. "I'm hungry, but I...I think we need to...to talk about a bunch of things."

"Of course we need to talk, but everything, including talking, is easier when your stomach isn't growling. Go ahead and put down a couple sandwiches and at least one bowl of soup." I don't wait to see if he starts eating; I just dig in. He watches me for a few seconds and does the same.

AFTER DINNER, WE get ready to turn in, and when we finally stretch out next to each other on the bed, Liam allows one of his long, noisy sighs.

"You ready to talk now?" I ask. The room is dark and cool, and the blankets are soft and warm on our naked bodies, creating the perfect condition for a powerful conversation, followed hopefully by equally vigorous sex. At least, that's my plan.

"Not really, but I know it's time." Liam snatches my hand and pulls it to his chest in a surprisingly needy gesture. He blurts out, "I knew I had to save *you* because I didn't save *her*."

I've never heard shrillness in his voice until now. My mouth falls open.

"I could hear her that night... Lucy was crying and calling my name...but I couldn't get to her." He has shifted into an almost catatonic monotone.

I want to ask him to start at the beginning, but if I stop him at this point, he may never start talking again. So I listen and let him relate the story in his own way.

"My bedroom door was hot... I felt it with the back of my hand like they taught us at school...and I knew I shouldn't open it. And there was smoke coming under the door. I had to go out the window...I had to...but I could hear her...poor Lucy...oh, Lucy..." Gradually, the monotone vanishes, and Liam sounds like a scared little boy. He makes a desperate choking sound. "I knew she was gonna die...and I left anyway because I was so scared...because *I* didn't want to die!"

I don't ask questions, and I don't pull him into my arms; I just squeeze the hand that's clutching mine to his chest. I want to remind him of what he once told me: you never know how you're going to act when you're terrified. But it isn't my time to talk.

"I jumped out the window...broke my leg that night...but I couldn't feel the pain until the next day. Mom and Dad...they were outside standing by the tree that we agreed would be our family meeting place if there was ever an emergency. And Mom and Dad..."

Remembering his parents at that critical moment eight years ago brings Liam to the point of sobs, and I urge, "Tell me the rest."

"Jase...when she saw me...when I got to the tree, Mom screamed, 'Where's my baby? Where's *Lucy*?' Then she asked how I dared to show my *fucking face* without my sister beside me, and she pushed me to the ground and kicked my belly again and again—until Dad pulled her off me—and then she pointed at the house and told me, 'Go back in there and get her!'"

"Liam..." Silent tears stream down my face. "Liam."

"And then Mom said I was fucking useless, and I always had been...and she ran into the house...Jase, it was burning...I could feel the heat from the flames all the way across the yard...and Dad had to chase her and drag her back out of there...and she was kicking and screaming and biting and pulling his hair..."

I'm horrified by the tragedy, and more specifically, by the torturous choice Liam had to make that night—to save himself or attempt to save his sister and likely die trying. And I'm furious with Donna for her cruelty and David for not standing up for his son, but, at the same time, I understand they all were in pain.

"I killed Lucy...can't you see? By jumping out the window to save myself, I caused her death!" Liam pulls his hand from mine and bolts up straight. "When Lucy died, our family died... I did this to all of us! And I want to go back...and do it again... I'd save her life or die trying!"

The truth is out: Liam feels responsible for Lucy's death. Sort of like how I feel responsible for Ginny's. But he had to deal with his guilt and grief and loss as a child...a child who lost his parents, for all practical purposes, on the very same night. "No, Liam, it's not your fault. You didn't kill her."

"And Jase, when I heard you whimper in the theater, it was as if I was right back in my bedroom on the night of the fire." Liam is determined to say what he needs to say, and even though it's hard to hear, I listen. "I had a chance to do the right thing with you. To make up for...what I let happen to my sister."

"But you did the right thing that night in your bedroom. You did what you were taught to do, and you escaped the fire with your life intact." I kneel behind him and drape my arms around his broad shoulders. "And if you'd left me in the theater, it would have been the right thing to do then, too."

"You can say those things, and you can think them...but I saw my mother's eyes when she told me she wished it was me who'd died in that fire!"

I pull him back onto the bed, and once he's lying beside me, I climb onto his chest. Seduction might not be the right thing to do at this moment, but it's the only thing I can come up with that will change the direction of his thoughts. He *needs* me to make love to him now. I bend and press my lips hard on his, and I keep them there until we're both gasping for breath. Then I say, "I needed you in the theater and I needed you at the hotel and I need you every day... I think somehow, some way, you were kept safe *for me.*"

Liam's arms quickly come around me, and he shifts my body beneath him. "And I needed to hear those words from you." I find myself gazing up into eyes less haunted, and more demanding. "I saved you and now I need to know you're mine."

His tears have dried, leaving streaks on his cheeks that add to a wild look I've never before seen. He speaks in a husky voice that's new to me too, and I'm stirred by the rawness and neediness he's allowing me to witness. "That's right, Liam, I'm yours."

"Tonight isn't going to be sweet or soft or tender, Jason. I'm gonna make sure you know you're mine..." He stops talking to pull in a deep breath. "I promise not to *hurt* you, but...what I do might *change* things." His hands encircle my wrists, and he weighs me down with his body, his burly chest pressing mine into the bed. He makes no effort to hide his hardness. "Now tell me you understand and this is what you want."

At first I just nod, but the glare he sends indicates he needs a verbal response. "Yes...it's what I want."

I'm spooked by his ferocity, but the troubled expression is absent from his eyes, and he's not withdrawn, as he'd been in the car. He's communicating, and it's honest communication. He's telling me what he needs from me. "I'll do anything... I'll do *everything* you want, okay?"

He nods once. "Then brace yourself." His order echoes in my mind, as it did when he suggested it once before.

A prickle of chills dances down the back of my neck and skirts around, landing on my nipples, which he's alternately sucking with such force I lose my breath. I resist the instinct to ask him to slow down so I can prepare myself, because I don't think I'll ever be ready for what he has in mind.

And in giving him what he wants, I'm going to get everything I need.

"So you've chosen to live by the honor code…you've heard of it, I'm sure. It goes like this—I saved your life, and now you owe me yours. Isn't that right?"

"I—I—uh…"

"I wanna be the one to guard your life." He starts to climb up my body. By the time he's seated on my chest, he's rambling, as if in a trance. "I need to know you're always gonna be safe, and here for me…so I need you to let me look out for you however I see fit…and I need to be able to take you…in bed…the way I want…because then I'll know you're really mine."

"Yes." This is all I have time to say.

Liam continues to climb my body until his dick is directly in front of my face. He paints my lips with its moist tip, and I know exactly what he wants. I slide my arms down to my sides, as he expects me to do. For a split second, I'm shocked, because never in my life did I envision myself in this position, or at least not on the bottom end of this situation. But I raise my mouth and feed on Liam's length the very second he lowers it to my lips. The sound he makes when I take him into my mouth is so gritty and primitive that it brings to mind a climax, but I have firsthand knowledge that this is not the case. I decide he's experiencing a different kind of release—a release of all the secrets and anguish and feelings of seclusion he's kept inside for far too many years.

He hovers over me, pushing himself in and out of my mouth, forcefully and repetitively, for so long I can't imagine how he can hold back his orgasm. His thrusts are rough and abrupt and purposeful; it seems he's unaware that it's me beneath him, struggling to guide his dick with my tongue in his frenzy of movement. But when he slows enough to reach down, softly caress my cheek, and say, "My Jase…my Jase,"

I know he remembers it's me who's under him. I take this moment to worship with my mouth, my lips, and my tongue, this man who keeps me safe, in body and soul, using a tender dominance I've come to crave.

Without warning, he stops what he's been so intent on doing. "Lie flat and open your legs." It's an order and I obey promptly. He turns around and descends onto my body in a heated rush. "I'm gonna have myself a feast. Don't squirm away from me...and..."

I'm not new to oral sex, but what Liam proceeds to do to me is in a category all its own. He's somehow harsh and at the same time gentle; I feel passion and fury with every stroke of his tongue and brush of his beard. On my body, he expresses his heartache at the loss of his family and his joy at finding me. I'm panting within a minute and shouting within two.

"Liam, let me touch you, too! Please, Liam!"

"I'll touch both of us!" In response to my begging, he throws himself on top of me, pushes our dicks together and grinds, kissing my lips with a hunger I'm not sure I can satisfy. Within a few seconds, we're both letting go, and it's so all-encompassing it almost hurts. The experience is too intense to actually keep kissing, so our mouths simply merge, wide open and pressed together, our tongues tangled, but unmoving.

After a full minute, he lifts his mouth from mine. Our faces are wet and chafed, as are our bodies, but it's perfect. "Tell me now," he utters, and I immediately know what he wants.

"I love you, Liam, and I'm yours."

He was right; everything is different now. I've given him full access to my body, and I'm glad.

And just like that, a soft sweet version of Liam is here. He snuggles down beside me, yawns, and says, "We're gonna seriously need showers in the morning, man." Just when I think I know Liam, he shows me a facet I've never before seen. "And I love you, too."

Chapter Twenty-One

I STILL SEE the haunted look on his face, but it only shows up every now and then since he confided in me what happened to his sister. I'm not naïve enough to think his problem with guilt and regret is suddenly resolved because he talked to me about it, and that residual pain from years of torturing himself about having left his sister in the house when it was on fire has miraculously disappeared, but having it all out in the open has taken away some of the power wielded by a big bad secret. So I guess I can say Liam's doing as well as can be expected under the circumstances. But I wish I could wipe all the agony away.

Classes, as well as our relationship, have been sailing along smoothly, which for some reason makes me worry. Maybe I've become a pessimist.

It's Columbus Day weekend. Batcheldor College's annual tradition is to welcome back alumni and all past students for Fall Festival. There's no shortage of activities on and off campus, and Liam and I are participating in the pumpkin-carving contest tonight. Batcheldor is also holding a theater exchange with some other schools where one-act plays will be performed in a judged competition at Harrison Theater. Mariah, Ginny's freshman year roommate and Liam's friend from the business program, is returning to Batcheldor to resurrect her part in last fall's production of *Oh, What a Tangled Web*. I'm not yet ready to go anywhere near that theater, even if Mariah is going to be there.

Last week, she reached out to both Liam and me by email, and the three of us settled on a time Saturday afternoon to meet at College Coffee on Main Street between her performances. This is as close to the theater as I'm willing to get.

Liam and I are sitting on high-backed wooden chairs in the coffee shop staring through its glass walls at the theater across the street. I don't know about Liam, but my mind is near to bursting with a resurgence of banished fears.

"Why did we agree to meet Mariah *here* of all places? This is a bad idea." I'm not ready to casually sip coffee in this close proximity to the Harrison Theater, nor am I prepared to have the *serious discussion* Mariah alluded to in her email.

Liam hooks his ankle around mine beneath the table, which helps me to feel marginally better. "We'll get through this, Jase. Just grab ahold of me if you're freaking out. I'm here for you, 'kay?"

This is yet another example of what I love about Liam. He's dependable and steady. Even when I feel *obligated* to worry, he lets me know that I won't be worrying alone. "Thanks...hey, look, she's here."

We both stand up to greet Mariah, and automatically reach out to hug her, but she steps away and avoids the physical contact. "Let's sit down," is all she says, her voice curt. She means business.

"We ordered you an iced chai latte, seeing as that was what you always brought with you to marketing class," Liam tells her. "Hope you're still into chai."

"It's fine." Mariah's blonde hair is slicked back in a tight bun, and she's wearing stage makeup that dulls the softness that would normally show on her pointy face. "I've got a bone to pick with you guys, and I'm here to get it off my chest."

I'm definitely not in the mood for *picking bones* with Mariah. Liam and I have had so many ups and downs in the past six months that all I want is to enjoy some peaceful, happy times with him and our friends. I thought tonight was going to be a bittersweet stroll down memory lane, talking about the good times with Ginny and how much we miss her, but it seems obvious I'm mistaken. Mariah has never been a person to keep her feelings boxed up, especially the negative ones. In fact, I remember Ginny saying Mariah could never let any minor problems be swept under the rug.

"Well, tell us what's wrong," I urge, although I'm pretty sure I don't want to know.

"You guys are *together* now, right?" She doesn't wait for either one of us to reply before adding, "Like you're *a loving couple*?"

Liam answers before I have a chance to. "We are. Do you have a problem with this, Mariah?"

Mariah's sky-blue eyes turn midnight-blue. "Maybe I do."

"And?" Liam's better than either Mariah or me at keeping his emotions under wraps. She's sneering, and I'm shaking, but Liam has leaned back in his chair and is stone-faced. "And what might your problem with us be?"

She doesn't hesitate to reply. "How about the fact that you guys aren't gay, and two straight guys screwing is disgusting and sick?"

I choke on a sip of cocoa, and Liam hands me a napkin, but other than that, neither of us responds. I literally can't; I'm too busy coughing. But Liam shakes his head slowly, biding his time, and waiting for more. Which he soon gets.

First, she glares at me. "Let's take you, Jason— you were oh-so-frigging-in-love with Ginny last year. I never heard a single word about you being unsure how you felt about her because you were gay!" The volume of Mariah's voice rises with every word. College Coffee is packed with students, who all stare our way. She shifts her angry gaze to Liam and even jabs her finger at him across the small table. "And you and me hooked up at that Marketing Club holiday party at Jarrod's place last winter. What the fuck was *that* if you're light in your loafers?"

I join Mariah in staring at Liam. He never told me anything was going on between them. He glances at me quickly—his expression unreadable—before responding to her. "That was a onetime thing, Mariah. You *know* that—we talked about it."

I'm floored by this revelation, but I don't blame him. We aren't required to confess every intimate detail of our lives, especially stuff that doesn't really matter. And unfortunately for Mariah, I think his hookup with her qualifies as inconsequential.

"How do you think it makes me feel to find out that the guy I was seeing and the guy my best friend was *hoping to marry* are gay for each other? Did you ever stop and think about that?"

Not only am I mildly shocked from learning that Liam and Mariah hooked up last year, but I also feel like a world-class piece of shit, because—*Ginny was hoping to marry me?* She never mentioned this! Maybe Mariah is confused; who wouldn't be in her shoes? I'm damned confused right now, too.

Liam doesn't seem to interpret this situation in the same way as Mariah. "Look, Mariah, we weren't 'seeing each other.' You and me had too many drinks and went too far at that party. I'm sorry it happened, because we're friends. But both of us know that's all it was... And as for Ginny and Jason, well, they *were* in love, but Ginny is...she's gone now."

"Jason was so in love with Ginny that he's fucking a dude *less than six months* after she died in his arms?"

I grit my teeth to help me cope with the sharp stab of guilt in my gut. The ugly truth is that Ginny didn't die in my arms; I let go of her right when she needed me most. She died, cold and alone on the floor of the theater.

Surprisingly, Liam seems unaware of my suffering. And he's patient enough to make one more effort to engage Mariah. "Think about this for a second, Mariah—Jason and I survived a *mass shooting* together, and the guy tried to come and finish us off a couple days later where we were in witness protection. Thanks to that living hell, the two of us bonded. Maybe we can't explain it—not that we're required to—but Jase and I don't wanna be apart."

"All I can say is, looking at your cozy little duo from the outside, everybody thinks you guys are mighty twisted." She stands up and crosses her arms in front of her— like my mother, unable to conceive of the concept of bisexuality. "I mean, *Jesus*, Liam…"

She's really mad, and I have no idea what she wants us to say or do. My head spins with images of Ginny and me— how close we'd once been and how we'd drifted apart as lovers. *Maybe I was gay all along…maybe my relationship with Ginny was nothing but a lie… And maybe Ginny was hurt and angry because she knew I didn't feel the same way she did, just like Mariah is feeling now. Or maybe I'm allowed to love who I love…and want who I want.* I fold my arms on the sticky table and drop my head onto them, once again utterly confused.

"Liam, come back to my hotel room…*alone*…and we can talk about this misunderstanding. We can sort it all out." Mariah's suggestion sends a jab of pain into my already throbbing belly. "I know how you like things, remember?"

She wants to "sort it all out" with my boyfriend. And she knows how he likes things? I stand up, too, and head for the door, because I can't just sit here and listen to her proposition Liam. And like an idiot, I trip on absolutely nothing, fall into Mariah, and nearly knock her onto her ass.

Liam is on his feet in an instant. He grabs my arm to steady me. "It's okay Jase... And Mariah, there's nothing for us to sort out."

"Liam—Jason just knocked *me* over, and you're jumping to *his* side?" I knew Mariah for almost a full year, and I never saw this bitter side of her.

Sometimes, I feel as if this *thing* with Liam simply can't work. There's too much going against it. And maybe Mariah's right—we aren't *really* bisexual men. We're just two straight guys...who don't belong together as a couple.

But I can't ignore the little voice in my head screaming at me and telling me *we do* fit together. It may not make sense to the rest of the world, but Liam and I work, romantically *and* sexually. Nonetheless, I don't plan to stand here and listen to any more. I turn and head for the door, which brings me face-to-face with the Harrison Theater. I stare through the glass at the building where every scrap of normalcy in my life was destroyed. But then, it was also the place where something incredible and precious was born.

This is all too much to deal with. I shudder violently, my entire body shaking. I push the glass door open and step outside. Standing on the sidewalk, nothing but the street between the theater and me, I get lost in the past. My heart pounds as I'm submerged in darkness, shots ringing out around me.

"Come on, Jase. It's time to go home." *I know this voice... I trust this voice.*

"Home?" I ask.

"Home...to my place." Liam takes me by the arm, gently and firmly, as he had a few minutes ago when I tripped. "Don't worry about Mariah. She was totally off base, and I told her so."

I let him lead me to his car. "You never told me you were with her."

Liam squeezes my arm. "It was one night. A mistake I never made again."

I nod because I think I understand. "Does she know how you *like things*?" I'm thinking about the way he dominates me in bed, and I wonder if he did the same to her. I secretly hope it's something he has wanted to do only with me, which I realize is a childish desire. A desire as strange as everything else going on here.

"No one but you knows how I like things. *I* didn't even know until the first night I was with you." Liam is burly and strong; he looks tough in his leather jacket and spiked hair and heavy boots. It would be easy to believe that the inner man is what he projects on the outside—dangerous. But that's not the case. Liam is gentle and protective, and I need him now...again...always, I think.

"I just want some 'normal' for a while. No shootings, no family drama, no interfering friends. Just time spent being...being boring," I tell him.

"You *know* your wish is always my command." He laughs, and the sound is a low roar. I place my hand on his chest so I can feel the rumble. "No pumpkin-carving contest featuring a round, orange Donald Trump, or wild parties, or drinking beer for us this weekend, man. It's pizza delivery and Netflix weekend. Your fine ass won't be getting up off my big bed."

"What'll you do to me if I decide to get off the bed to clean your kitchenette?" I smirk.

"Just try it and see." He winks. "It's time for some 'normal' in our lives. Prepare to be bored as hell."

I laugh and take his hand in mine. "Promises, promises."

We walk past the theater and around the building to the parking lot where our very normal chariot—if you count red Dodge Chargers as normal—awaits.

Chapter Twenty-Two

I ASKED FOR normalcy, and Liam delivered. We spent the remainder of last weekend lounging around his apartment. We studied a little, watched plenty of movies, and consumed far too much pizza and soda. It was great in a very ordinary way, which was just what I needed. But it wasn't even slightly boring.

More normalcy: Club soccer games are on Wednesday nights, and BJ and I have standing running dates on Tuesday and Thursday afternoons, as soon as classes end. We meet in our dorm, change quickly into running gear, and are out the door within ten minutes because BJ works restacking books at the Batcheldor College Library most weeknights from six until nine.

Today, as we stretch out on a scanty patch of yellow autumn grass in front of RetroHouse, BJ and I catch up on what's been going on.

"So Dacia wants me to go home with her for Thanksgiving."

"Doesn't she live in Florida? Sounds like a mini-vacation to me."

BJ isn't laughing and joking as usual. In fact, he seems terrified. "I can't go... I can't meet her parents, cuz Jase—they're lawyers. They'll see right through my bullshit line and know that I'm no good for their daughter."

My right calf is tight, and I rub it hard with a pink rubber ball I keep in the pocket of my sweats whenever I go running. "BJ, you aren't so much full of shit as you are a colorful kind of guy with a lot to say...about everything."

"Yeah...like I said, I'm full of shit. I know it, and you know it, but Dacia doesn't." BJ drops to the cold ground in a defeated pile of limbs.

"Get up, BJ. Dacia's nuts about you. So you should go home with her and meet her folks...and while you're there, soak up the sun. The trip will move you into a more serious zone in the relationship."

"You met Liam's folks. Did that move you forward in your relationship?"

I shake my head, remembering the severely dysfunctional family I met in Lockwood, Maine. "I think his family falls into a unique category called 'major exception to the rule.' But my mom met Liam and fell in love with him and *that* moved us forward. As in, I have some serious competition for my boyfriend's attention with my mother. He's coming to my house for Thanksgiving. It's already settled."

"Your mom just accepted that you're all of a sudden gay?" BJ knows how to get to the heart of a matter. "I'm pretty sure my folks would have something to say if I woke up one morning and told them I was into dudes."

I get onto my feet and bend down to stretch my hamstrings. "You ready to run now?" There's a good chance BJ wouldn't understand that we love and want each other—*ever heard of being bi, dude?* Liam and I have come to embrace this, but I'm not in the mood to explain it, especially since I don't know how. It just is.

"Yeah...you go on ahead and set the pace."

I start running slowly down the side of the country road, thinking about Liam. It seems I'm constantly trying to explain, to myself and others, the exact nature of my feelings for him. *How can I have fallen in love with Liam when before him I was only interested in women? How can sex feel so good with him when I used to believe only a girl's body could provide me with pleasure?*

I turn up Main Street and head for the first set of lights, so deep in thought I'm only half aware of my surroundings. I find it hard to explain in words, but I can't deny that I love him. When it comes down to the barest of facts, I love a *human being*, and I'm into his body as much as his mind. Maybe Liam and I are the only ones who are able to see love clearly—we love for how we feel in our partner's presence: secure, protected, and treasured. And we're compelled to be together. When we touch each other, it's because we can't *not* touch each other.

It really isn't so complicated at all.

When BJ catches up with me, I'm ready to tell him the truth. "I don't much care if his parents or my friends or Mariah Craft thinks it's fucked up that Liam and I are together." I'm running at a good clip now, so I take a few deep breaths before I continue. "My sexuality hasn't changed—I'm just more aware of it now because my life experience *has* changed. Radically. Shit, I almost got killed twice, BJ. And loving Liam works with how I fit into the world."

BJ slaps my shoulder and pouts noticeably. "Hey, chill out! I wasn't putting you down, dude! It was just an innocent question."

"No hard feelings... I guess I'm still reacting to our meeting with Mariah."

"This morning, Liam told me she was super pissed at you guys."

"Yeah...but I think a lot of it was because she felt as if she needed to defend Ginny's honor...and then there's the part where she still has a thing for Liam."

We're far enough along in our run where the gab session has to end, and it's time to get serious. I sprint out ahead of BJ and focus on my inspiration: Liam Norcross, who just happens to be pumping iron in the Batcheldor College Gymnasium.

Chapter Twenty-Three

"YOU'RE NO MONSTER," I whisper when he rolls off me, both of us sweaty and satisfied, but I see that troubled expression in his eyes.

"You're no monster," I say as he gently pushes me beneath the spray of hot water, after soaping up my entire body in his usual attentive manner. Because I can see the suffering on his face.

"You're no monster," I tell him between spoons full of butterscotch ice cream that he's feeding me in the ice cream parlor downtown, because his guilt is showing again.

"You are not a monster, Liam." Time and again, he hears these words from me, because I know he hasn't fully forgiven himself for something that doesn't even require forgiveness. All he did was save himself instead of die trying to save his little sister. I plan to give him the absolution he thinks he needs, which his parents refused him.

And Liam still won't open up fully about the details of the night he lost his little sister. Last time I brought it up, he said, "You know what happened on the night of the fire. I'm not trying to hide anything from you, but it hurts like hell to even think about, so there's no way I can talk about it."

I step into the shower and think about how far *I've* come in six months. Although I still experience some posttraumatic symptoms from the shooting and the subsequent attempt on our lives—like feeling panicked when I hear sudden loud noises and trying to avoid small, enclosed public spaces—I'm back to being a reasonable facsimile of Jason Tripp. And every day, I hope it will be the day Liam allows my supportive words to sink into his brain. But I'm especially hopeful this morning, because today marks six months since the Harrison Theater shooting.

"I owe so much to Liam." I say it aloud, the water dripping into my mouth as I speak. "I can help him feel better, the way he helped me."

I END THE call and put my cell phone down on the desk where I'm sitting, studying Media Law and trying not to dwell on how it's been half a year to the day since my life changed so dramatically. "Okay, BJ. I talked to Liam, and we decided we're going to go see Dacia at the Volunteer Entertainers Show tonight." I really want to support Dacia's efforts at raising money for local homeless families, but the decision to enter a theater—even if it's the Oakwood downtown and not the Harrison—has been a tough one for me.

"So Liam worked his magic and got you to say you'd go?" BJ never takes a subtle approach.

Liam and I have been going back and forth about whether or not to attend the show all day, until finally I agreed.

BJ is dressed in black because he's working as a stagehand at the event. "Awesome. And speaking of magic, Dacia's been taking magic lessons at the Community Center since school started to get ready. She's gonna be so psyched you'll be there! You said Liam's coming too, right?"

Hello! Like I would actually consider entering a theater without Liam...

"Yeah, I'm going to meet him in front of Charlie's Steakhouse, and we'll go across the street to the theater as soon as he gets there." I swallow hard as I'm still struggling with this decision. I'm honestly afraid. "But Liam might be a little late meeting me because he has a Marketing Club meeting until seven. So we'll probably miss the first couple of acts."

"Dacia's magic act is second to last in the show, so you guys should be fine." He pulls a black sweater over his T-shirt. "Okay, so I'll see you at the theater, and maybe afterward we can all grab a bite to eat downtown. And fair warning—if you sit too close to the front of the stage, Dacia might pick you for the audience participation section."

"Then we'll be in the back row, for sure. And tell Dacia good luck, or, maybe *break a leg* is more correct."

"Will do... See ya later, Tripp."

As soon as BJ leaves the room, I place my head between my knees. The mere thought of setting foot in a dark theater makes me feel queasy.

THE SCENE AT Charlie's Steakhouse is totally chaotic when I arrive. I thought the walk from campus would do me good, maybe even clear my head, but not in my wildest dreams did I expect to see people streaming out of the theater, screaming that there's a fire. As soon as I notice that many of the theatergoers are children, my thoughts turn to Liam. *How is he going to react when he gets here—to a fire in a place where there are children present?* A tragic fire is his biggest fear, and to compound it, the fire is in a theater. And we both reacted badly to the fatal arson in the Imax theater that we heard about on the news a few weeks ago.

As the horror sinks into my brain, I lose myself to fear. This is the type of situation I've dreaded since last April. My thoughts stray to terrifying gunmen and hooded arsonists, and, shaking, I drop to my knees on the sidewalk. Alarmed that no rescue vehicles are here yet, I manage to pull my phone from my pocket and dial 911 to report the fire.

"Jase! Jase!" It's Liam. He isn't coming from the direction of the theater parking lot, but from down the street in the opposite direction. "You okay?" Before I can answer, he stops in front of me, bends down and runs his hands over my body, starting with my face, from my neck to my shoulders, then right down my arms to my fingertips. He refuses to believe I'm okay unless he checks for himself.

"I'm freaking out! I called 911 and—" I stop short when I notice Liam is as pale as a ghost. And his expression—it's not haunted, as I expect. He seems wired.

Thin billows of smoke stream from the theater's double doors. The few people who are still straggling out are soaking wet, and most hold jackets over their mouths.

A woman carrying a baby girl, and holding the hand of a little boy, rushes up to Liam and me. "Oh, God! My daughter...she was right behind me but now... Now I don't know where she is! Oh, God! I told her to follow me, and... Oh, God! Please help me!"

The mother starts to sway, and I think she may be suffering from smoke inhalation. I jump to my feet and she stuffs the baby into my arms, rasping, "Hold onto my son..." She stares plaintively at Liam. "...and find my daughter, Sara!!" And then she's on the ground, her eyes half-closed. Having never held a baby before, I struggle with the squirming bundle, and at the same time, try to grasp the hand of a little boy wailing, "Mama!"

When I look to Liam for help, I see a stubborn expression on his face that horrifies me. "No...no, Liam..." My voice is low and quiet, but he knows exactly what I mean. But just in case, I spell it out. "You can't go in there."

"I...I have to... *You know* I've gotta find this lady's little girl!" Our gazes meet, and the connection is powerful. It's as if a bolt of lightning has shot directly from Liam's eyes and struck me. We're more connected than ever before and at the same time more isolated. Part of me wants to nod—to give him my blessing to enter the burning building so he can save the little girl—but it's more than I can ask of myself.

I have to dissuade him because I can't lose him. "Listen, Liam, hear the sirens? The fire department is on their way and...you'll probably only get in the way if you go in there."

But he doesn't hear my final argument because he's already on his way into the building, screaming, "Sara! Sara! I'm not gonna leave you!"

Standing here on the sidewalk, juggling a wiggly baby and clutching the hand of a terrified little boy, there's no way I can follow him inside. I rise to the occasion and steady the baby in my arm, kneel down to comfort the little boy, and try to figure out whether their mother has had a heart attack.

But I've never felt more alone in my life. Never.

AS SOON AS the police and firefighters arrive, the bystanders are moved off the sidewalk and herded into a nearby parking lot. Once the mother and her children I helped are being examined by EMTs, I tell a nearby firefighter that my boyfriend is in the building searching for a little girl named Sara. She assures me they're doing everything possible to rescue all of the people from the building.

I stare at the Oakwood Theater, thinking that it's not aptly named; it's a brick building. I see no flames and little in the way of smoke, but I know that what's going on inside could be as devastating as what happened on my last visit to a theater. And the person who saved me from death and subsequent depression—a man who defines my future—is in that building, fighting the demons of his past. I pull mercilessly at my short hair, unable to cope with the possibility of losing Liam to another tragedy.

I make my way to the front of the parking lot where I plant my feet and stare, my eyes glued to the wide entrance to the theater. And although I have no idea how to pray, I find a way. I pray with everything inside me that the next person I'll see coming from the theater doors will be Liam. But my prayers aren't answered.

How long can someone be inside a smoky, burning building without oxygen...and survive? It's been at least ten minutes since Liam left me, maybe more. *Let him be okay, let him be okay, I need him, I need him...*

The vicinity of the theater is buzzing with action—firefighters, police, and EMT's bravely do their jobs, news reporters set up and speak grimly into the cameras in various corners of the parking lot, some adults hug children and others wait anxiously for loved ones who are still unaccounted for. And like so many times before, I'm frozen with fear. I want everyone to be okay, of course, and I worry for BJ and Dacia. I worry for the poor woman's little girl, Sara, and for all of the other children trapped in the theater. But the person who is my future is in that building, trying his best to be a hero, as he's compelled to do. Liam is sacrificing his life for a little girl he doesn't know because he thinks he failed in saving the life of another little girl he loved so much.

And so I wait. Every minute seems to last forever.

When I finally see him emerge from the theater, sooty and staggering, the limp body of a little girl in his arms, I again drop to my knees in the parking lot. I watch as the little girl is taken from his arms and rushed to an ambulance, and then Liam is led behind a wall of uniformed people, where I can't see him anymore.

Liam is alive. This time, his battle with the demons that haunt his mind didn't kill him. *But what about next time?*

What about next time?

Chapter Twenty-Four

IN MY ENTIRE life, I've never been angrier with anyone than I am right now. From my distant spot, kneeling in the parking lot across the street from the theater, I watch closely as my boyfriend is loaded into an ambulance—an oxygen mask strapped to his face—and whisked away. I'm overwhelmed by panic that's inspired by fear of losing him to another tragic event, coupled with yet another of his attempts to be a hero. It's more than I can handle.

I don't stop running until I'm standing in front of the door to my room. I knock and push the door open without listening for BJ's voice telling me it's okay to come in. He and Dacia are on his bed, thankfully dressed, and I yell, "Get outta here—I need to be alone—I'm sorry, but *go!*"

"My man...whassup? You pissed cuz the show got canceled? I tried to call, but you didn't answer. And there was so much confusion around the theater. I guess some of the people in the audience got stuck in there for a while." BJ is rambling as if he feels really bad I missed his girlfriend do a frigging magic act. He approaches me and lifts his arm to pat my back, but I slap first. Then I take a swing at BJ's arm, and when I miss, I take a badly aimed swing at his face, but BJ easily blocks it. "Hey, what's the matter, man? I can't help that something electrical got fucked-up in the theater and started smoking. Don't blame me. I called you as soon as they told the performers and stagehands to leave...but, no worries, the show's gonna get rescheduled."

"Jeez, BJ, I had no idea Jase was *so* into magic," Dacia adds.

Pop-pop-pop...

And I'm back in the theater... It's pitch-black and the sound of gunshots makes me jump...I'm shaking and sweating, and I can't find Ginny.

"Ginny, where are you? Ginny? Fuck! Where are you, Ginny?"

Lying flat on the cold, sticky floor, I reach around for her, but I can't find her, so I squeeze my eyes shut and curl up into a ball under the seats and I wait for Liam's heavy body to press down on me and shelter me from the gunfire, but he never comes.

"I swear he thinks he's back in the Harrison Theater, Dacia...just look at him."

"You might be right...this is *too* weird."

"Dude...dude...you aren't in that theater! Shit, Dacia...should we call health services? What do ya think?"

"I don't know...but he's totally losing it, BJ."

"Liam!" I call.

"Where *is* Liam?" BJ asks.

"I hope Liam's not as disappointed as Jase about the show being canceled," Dacia offers casually.

Dacia's senseless remark starts to break me out of my flashback. I'm finally able to open my eyes. I'm in my dormitory room, curled up in a ball on the floor beside my bed. "Liam." I have no idea why I say his name again.

BJ and Dacia help me up off the floor and onto my bed. At this point, BJ seems to catch on that something is seriously wrong. "Dude, what the fuck is going on with you?"

My voice shaking, I say, "We got there at seven...people were screaming and running out of the theater because there was a fire."

"There wasn't a fire. Just a ton of smoke," Dacia corrects me. "So, for the record, there isn't always fire where there's smoke."

I'm astounded by her inability to recognize the seriousness of this situation. "Liam went in to save a little girl. She was lost, and her mother asked him to go find her...and I told him not to go, but he went anyway."

"Well, shit. Your boyfriend is either stupid or a hero." BJ is about as clueless as his girlfriend. Even in my distraught state, I admit they're freakishly well matched.

I go on with my story, hoping they'll get the picture that, after the performers left, things got pretty dicey at the Oakwood Theatre. "We could hear the sirens...I told him help was coming...but he went into the theater."

"Well, where the fuck is Liam now?" BJ is beginning to see the seriousness of a situation he thought was just a minor inconvenience.

"They took him in an ambulance... I need you guys to find him for me. But don't bring him back here." I yawn. And then I yawn again. The same twisted response I experienced after the theater shooting is happening to me now. My eyelids feel heavy; I can't stay awake. I'm so exhausted I have to close my eyes, but I need to know that BJ and Dacia will find Liam.

I don't want them to bring him back here to me. I want them to take him home to his apartment and make sure he's okay...to stay with him and take care of him until he's better. But not to bring him back to me, because I'm not the same guy Liam saved six months ago. I'm a guy who survived hell, more than once, and I need to move on from that place of loss and suffering.

And Liam is a loose cannon when it comes to his need to be a hero. I don't know if he'll ever be able to stop himself from trying to save everybody, right and left, and reliving these brushes with death that must somehow prove to him he has the right to be alive. Maybe I'm wrong...maybe I'm exaggerating because I'm scared. Or maybe I just want to be safe and to know Liam is safe and...and I don't know if this is possible.

As soon as I close my eyes, I'm slammed by sleep's oblivion.

"HEY, JASE...WAKE up. Liam sent me back here to look after you." It's Dacia, and for once, she's making sense. "He wants me to tell you he's okay. He was checked by a doctor who said he suffered some smoke inhalation, but then gave him some oxygen and released him from the hospital."

I yawn. Waking up is close to impossible with this weird sleeping affliction I have in times of stress, but it becomes easier to open my eyes when I feel as if I'm going to be sick. I dive for the trashcan beside the bed and heave, but nothing comes up.

Nonetheless, Dacia squeals, "Ewwww!"

It's hard to believe she's in the nursing program at Batcheldor. "Yeah, I know." I tuck the trashcan into the corner and sit up, sliding my legs over the edge of the bed. I take a deep breath and say, "I'm glad Liam is okay."

"I didn't say he was okay."

"You said they released him..."

"He's okay, like medically...but not in his head, you get what I'm saying, hon? The dude is like...desperate. Because we told him you don't want to see him."

"He wants to see me?"

"Um...*yeah!*" Dacia sits down beside me. "BJ basically had to tie him to the bedpost to keep him from coming here."

The reality of our situation is clear to me, and I have an important decision to make. I know that Liam is mine in heart and soul, and even in body, but when someone, and I mean *anyone*, needs a hero, he will always be more theirs than mine. And I don't know if I can live with this prospect.

"I can't see him right now. I'm not ready. I need to think. I..." I'm rambling. "I need you and BJ to keep him away from me because... it's over with us."

Part Four

November

Chapter Twenty-Five

MAYBE I'M THE most selfish person in the world to break up with a guy for being a hero. But I know one thing: I can't love him as much as I do and then risk losing him if I don't absolutely have to. But this is exactly what I did. And I didn't even do it the honorable way: face-to-face over a steak dinner and a few sorrowful glasses of red wine. I told Dacia to tell Liam that it's over. Because I'm done.

I don't know how things are going for him, but this break up isn't working out very well for me. As is typical, on Saturday morning, I run home to my mother with my tail between my legs, having no idea what I expect her to do to make me feel better. In fact, her "Mom knows best/Mom knows all" attitude is nearly insufferable, on a good day. But it's also all I know. It's familiar, like the old pair of scratchy wool socks she gave me for Christmas in tenth grade; they're always there when I need them to prevent a case of frostbite, but even as they keep me warm, they're irritatingly itchy, to the point of being nearly intolerable. And maybe because Liam's behavior, in terms of heroism, isn't predictable, I require a taste of my familiarly irritating home life.

"There's far too much drama going on in the theaters near your college, dear. You would have been wise to have transferred out of Batcheldor this summer."

I wonder if Mom realizes that what goes on in theaters is *supposed* to be dramatic. "There wasn't even an actual fire, Mom. Just some electrical problems that led to a lot of smoke."

"That's nothing but a minor detail…" She places a bowl of pasta sprinkled with veggies in front of me on the kitchen table and then pops open my can of soda. "So tell your mother what your friend Liam did that caused you to run home without him, not that I'm disappointed to see you."

I'm not hungry for Mom's Double Veggie Pasta Primavera, and I'm not up for this conversation, but since I voluntarily put myself in her line of fire, so to speak, it's my duty to respond. "Liam can't look the other way when someone needs to be rescued. He's willing to risk his life and…Mom, I'm not willing to let him risk it."

Mom places the can beside my plate and sits down across from me. "Not to be argumentative, because you know that's not my way, but you met Liam *only because* he saved your life."

I don't know how she can keep a straight face, trying to pass herself off as politely agreeable, but I don't call her on it.

"And tell me if I'm wrong, but before you met Liam, it was always girls, girls, girls for you… Something about Liam made that status change. Some quality in that boy…well, I'm not sure it *turned* you gay, but it made you unable to look away from him."

I'm amazed how clearly my mother sees the situation between Liam and me, even if she doesn't understand that people can be attracted to both men and women. I'd wondered how she rationalized it all. As it turns out, she saw what was right before her eyes and simply took it at face value: the near-death experiences I shared with Liam opened my mind to the fullness of my capacity to bond with another human being. *Wonders never cease.*

"You liked what you saw in him. Enough to… Son, you liked him well enough to bring him home to meet me. That says a lot."

I roll my eyes and dig into the pasta, hoping it will excuse me from responding.

Mom, however, hasn't lifted her fork. "Did you fall for him because of his bravery...his compassion, maybe? Or was it his dependability, strength, patience, and kindness?"

Her point is clear—I love the heroic qualities of Liam Norcross—and I'm pretty sure her questions are rhetorical. But they make me think, which, apparently, was the point. "Point taken."

Mom folds her hands on her lap and presses her lips together primly. She then delivers a line she must have learned from me. "Just saying, dear. And put your napkin on your lap."

Her point is that I fell in love with the man who saved me, time and again. I fell in love with my hero...and I was never happier than when I was taking care of him, largely by letting him take care of me. Being a hero is, in part, Liam's nature, but it became more prominent in his character after years of chastising himself thanks to his parents' treatment of him after his sister's death.

If we are to go on and build a future together, I must accept that a combination of nature and nurture causes Liam to be a compulsive hero.

LYING IN BED, I toss and turn, knowing that if Liam were near, I'd drape myself across his burly chest and be fast asleep in seconds. Liam is probably tossing and turning in his own bed right now, and it hurts to acknowledge this.

My phone buzzes. It's after midnight, so I'm both surprised and alarmed. I pick it up and read the text.

Liam: *I miss having you in my bed so much, Jase. I think I'll sleep on the futon tonight.*

Jase: *I miss you too. But I just don't think it's safe for me to stay with you and grow closer to you. I'm afraid I won't be able to live without you if I lose you to your heroics.*
Liam: *You're living without me right now.*
Jase: *When you risk your life, you also risk my heart.*
Liam: *I'm so sorry.*
Jase: *I don't know what to say...*
Liam: *I do. I love you. Night.*

My heart does this crunching-up thing I didn't know was possible, and if I weren't suffering serious emotional trauma right now, I'd go to the emergency room to check it out. But the pain comes from the simple fact that he's there, and I'm here, and it's by my choice, and I'm not sure if it's a permanent situation.

I DECIDE IT'S in my best interest to skip classes, at least for the beginning of this week, but I went about it in a responsible manner. I emailed all my professors and told them I'd been at the Oakwood Theatre downtown where there had been an emergency situation on Friday night and, thanks to my experiences at Harrison Theater last spring, I needed some time to deal with my emotions. The professors were all very kind and allowed me the time off. But what I really need to sort out is whether I can continue to love a hero.

Mom is at work today, which comes as a relief. I don't have to pretend I'm okay and that being separated from Liam isn't tearing me apart. I guess I hadn't realized what a friend he'd become. Sure, our relationship has blossomed significantly in the sex and romance department, which had originally been my biggest concern, but our friendship started on the night he saved me at the theater, and it has grown, as well. I had no idea how much his daily presence meant to me, until now.

So, what do I choose to do with my solitary freedom? I stretch out on the very same couch on which I spent the better part of the summer wasting away. And I think and remember. I weigh and measure.

The memory of Liam's eyes is vivid; I close mine and picture him gazing at me...studying me. In the past I always laughed when guys said things like "her eyes could see into my soul, dude," but Liam's truly can.

"Shit, if I worship the guy this much after knowing him for barely six months, how would I survive if he decided to rescue a bunch of nuns from a fiery bus crash and died doing it?" I'm alone in our house, so it makes no difference if I speak aloud, which I do. "I'm no good at dealing with stress without Liam. And if he was ever gone for good because he sacrificed his life saving someone we didn't even know... Well, I couldn't deal with that."

On the coffee table beside the couch, my phone buzzes.

Liam: *Missing my guy today.*

Jase: *You aren't alone.*

Liam: *Last night in bed I was thinking...part of what you love about me is that I'm a hero—you always tell me that I'm your hero. How can I stop being who I am?*

Jase: *I know who you are. I love who you are. That's the problem.*

Liam: *How can loving me be a problem?*

I have no answer for this.

Liam: *Let me just come and see you. We can talk. I can hold you.*

Jase: *Part of loving you right now means keeping my distance from you.*

I can't decide something this huge while looking into his eyes and listening to his voice. I need to be alone.

Jase: *And you need to stop texting me, Liam. I broke up with you because loving you hurts. Give me some space.*

I can practically hear his pained gasp and see his watery eyes. But I put the phone down and decide it's time to go for a run.

I HAVEN'T BEEN this much of a wreck since last summer. On my run, I suspect every driver of each car that passes of having a secret desire to run me down. When my mother drops a brownie pan on the kitchen floor, I run for cover behind the reclining chair. A dog barks in the yard next door, and I leap to the window in search of blue lights. I'm not doing well.

I'm not doing well without Liam.

Mom comes into the room and sits beside me on the couch. "How long are you planning on staying home? I love having you here, but you must be missing a lot of classes."

"I figure I'll go back on Wednesday. Or Thursday, maybe."

She pats me on the knee. "Pardon the expression, but you are a hot mess without your friend Liam." The timer goes off in the kitchen, but the awesome smell signifies the brownies are done. "I'm not *telling* you to go back to Batcheldor on Wednesday, Jason, but I really think you should go back sooner, rather than later."

"Point taken." I experience déjà vu because this isn't the first time I've spoken these words to Mom this week. Looks as if I'll be going back to school on Wednesday.

IT'S BEEN FIVE days since we last saw each other and, this time, Liam has not given up on me as he did last summer. After a half-day text hiatus on Monday, Liam's messages resume. I get texts from him...pretty much hourly. They inform me that he loves me. That I'm his priority. That he would never choose to save another above me because he is *my* hero. That I'll always come first in his mind, in every way. And the weird thing is, I believe him. And I've surprised myself by responding to each and every one of his texts, but maybe not in exactly the way he wants. Especially when he asks would I please just talk to him face-to-face? Because, like I told him, part of loving him right now requires me to keep my distance, and if I communicate with him at all, it's by using neither eyes nor smiles nor voices nor bodies. But I've allowed the stripped-down texting method of word exchange.

I'm not heartless. I'm not cruel. And I love Liam more than I ever knew it was possible to love another person. I think the fact that I've had to come to grips with the truth of my sexuality has allowed me to see him more clearly, to know him more thoroughly, and to love him more completely.

Another text from Liam comes in. According to his class schedule, he's texting me in his weekly Info Systems Workshop.

Liam: *Are you back at school now?*

Jase: *Yeah. I'm in my dorm. This might seem random, but there's an old song Billy, Don't Be a Hero. Ever hear it?*

Liam: *Maybe I heard it a long time ago. My parents used to have some oldies records, back before the fire.*

Jase: *Well, the song is about a girl who begs this guy named Billy not to be a hero when he goes off to fight in a war. So he can come home to marry her.*

Liam: *Is this a proposal? LOL*

Jase: *I just mean that I'm not the only one who feels this way, and who wants the one he loves to stop trying to save everybody else, and to just save himself.*

Liam: *I don't need to save myself. The way you love me saves me every day.*

After a short pause, another message.

Liam: *And I promise, Jase. I'll come home to marry you.*

Jase: *OMG. Come to my dorm after class. Okay?*

Liam: *I'll be right there. And I mean right there...cuz I'm at your door now. And I talked to BJ. The room is ours for the whole afternoon.*

I hear a soft knocking.

Am I ready for this? Have I decided how...or if...I'm going to let Liam back into my life?

I open the door before the third knock and stare at him. He looks better than ever before, but that could be because I missed him so much. Not only is he wearing a crisp black jacket and a dark plaid bow tie, but his hair is pushed off his face in soft spikes, to indie rocker perfection. Plus, he's wearing my favorite pair of butt-hugging jeans. And he's holding a dozen long-stemmed red roses, partially hiding the sexiest pout ever.

"I've never received flowers before," I admit softly. My voice breaks twice in this short sentence.

"Another first for us." He steps through the doorway, places the flowers on a shelf, and takes me in his arms. "Oh, yeah... this is where you belong."

"That's exactly what I was thinking...about you." I reach up and drape my arms around his rugged shoulders.

"I promise I'll never foolishly risk my safety again, Jase. My life with you means way too much to me."

"I'm going to hold you to that promise."

"What I did the other night had a lot to do with my little sister," Liam confesses, but I already know this. "I've been thinking about Lucy this week, and how my family allowed the loss of her to affect our lives. Being with you has definitely short-circuited my pain—you make me feel more at peace than I ever have before. Sometimes I tell you that you saved me as much as I saved you, and it's true, but I've decided that I'm going to go to the College Counseling Center. I've lived with a lot of guilt about Lucy's death, and so much pain because of how my parents treat me—I don't need to live this way. And I don't want to make you live this way."

"I think counseling is a good idea. It's helped me a lot." Now I'm going to say what really needs to be said. "I'm sorry I shut you out this week. I really needed some space to think."

"I was hopeful you'd let me back in, but what you did, staying away, gave me the time to realize that I live my life like I owe it to Lucy to save the world. I need to deal with Lucy's death, once and for all."

"We both had issues to sort out this past week, and I think we did. But...are you trying to tell me that I did you a *big favor* by refusing to see you? Because I could go home for a few more days." I blink up into his eyes a couple of times in an attempt to appear perfectly innocent.

Liam laughs. "I wouldn't go that far...because it hurt not being able to hold you last week. But you're right—I needed space to come to terms with everything I've lost, and what I've gained too." He releases me from his arms, keeping hold of my hands. "But I also know there's no way two people can love each other the way we do and not ultimately end up together. Does that make sense?" Before I answer, Liam lets go of my hands and approaches my bed. "I'd like you to lie down flat on your bed. On your back. Am I gonna get what I want?"

Still overwhelmed by the fact we're here together, it starts to hit me that Liam is already moving us in the direction of reconnecting in bed.

"What are you waiting for, Jason? Get on the bed." I can tell he's fighting an urge to smile because he wants to shift our reunion into a higher gear.

I scramble to the bed.

"Lie flat."

I do.

"You know I love you." He sits on the edge of the bed, staring into my eyes. "And I want your body, but not because it's perfect and sexy and the best body at Batcheldor College, which it is, but because it belongs to you. And *you* belong to me."

That's all he has to say to get me hard and ready for whatever he has in mind. I like it that he decides what we do in bed. And he likes it that he decides, too. I can tell by his leer.

"You have *way* too many clothes on, Jase." And then his hands are on me. They're rough and needy, stripping me down more than undressing me.

"You left my socks on," I say when he smiles down at me as if he's well pleased with my naked body.

"Maybe I want your socks on."

"Or maybe not...you're addicted to my feet." Even though serious intensity is sexy, I love it when we laugh together during sex, which we're doing right now.

"Maybe so." Liam reaches down and pulls my socks off, one by one. "I should start by tickling you—it'd serve you right." But instead, he lifts one foot with his hand and takes my toes into his mouth.

I'm getting more turned on by the second, but I still tease him. "You have a lot of faith in me."

He stops sucking and examines me quizzically. "How so?"

"You trust that I washed my feet this morning." And with those words, Liam strips off his clothes with the same vigor that he removed mine, and is on top of me, staring into my eyes. I've never seen so much love in my life as I see in his dark gaze.

Today, when he makes love to me, it's not with demands that I stay still. I know what he likes— when I keep my hands by my side, when I arch my back when I come, when I tell him I'm his after he comes—and he knows I'll do these things for him. Just as I know he'll take his time and be careful to prepare me, and hold me until I'm finished with my climax.

He lifts my chin and gazes into my eyes. "I want you to look at me...in the eyes...from beginning to end of this. Do you understand?"

I nod.

"I'd like to hear your answer."

"Yes. I'll look at you."

"I may have to look away when I'm getting you ready, but you're not to take your eyes from my face."

"Okay, Liam."

I fix my eyes on his as he grips my dick and starts to jerk. I slip quickly into heaven and have to concentrate on looking at him. When he places his dick against mine, licks his big palm and rubs them as if they're one, all I want to do is squeeze my eyes shut. "Don't look away." It's a struggle to stay focused, but it's worth it when I see the expression in his eyes. Passion, ownership, tenderness, and, of course, the backbone of our relationship, love, are all visible there. He releases us.

"I'm going to get some things we need from the drawer by the bed. Don't look away." I study his handsome face as he reaches for the condoms and lube. He seems young today, very boyish—he is as lost in his passion as a child playing with toy trucks in the sand. And then his eyes are back on mine. He kneels between my legs and lifts my ass onto his thigh, and watches my face very closely as he penetrates me with his fingers. I can feel his dick against my thigh. Its presence is a constant reminder of what I need to prepare myself to accept.

"Can I close my eyes?" I ask when he touches a certain spot inside me that makes me feel like exploding.

"You know the answer to that question." His eyes search mine as his fingers invade me, and I see more desire in his expression than ever before. He shakes his head slowly and says, "I need to put a condom on, Jason. Now watch my eyes as I do this."

I nod, and my gaze clings to his as he opens the small package and unrolls the condom on his sturdy erection.

He pushes my legs apart and then separates me enough to enter, and once again, the battle between his dick and my ass begins. As he pushes inside, I dare to blink a split second too long for Liam's liking, and he demands, "Eyes on me." And our gazes are again connected.

I see such vulnerability in his expression as he drives into me suddenly and deeply, which I don't expect at all. It's a paradox—a blend of tenderness and aggressiveness—that's unique to Liam. So badly, I want to raise my hand to touch his cheek, and I tell him. "I want to touch your face."

He replies, "Touch me with your eyes."

And I do. I let the love in my heart pour out through my eyes, and I can tell by his gentle smile he feels it. Without glancing away, he takes my dick in his hand and squeezes it firmly to let me know he's going to start to pleasure me, and his hand begins to move.

"We were never really apart." This is what he says just before his thrusts become more powerful and his wrist moves with the same commanding rhythm. His dark eyes challenge me to deny this, but I can't.

I know he's right. Trading a week of eating meals together and lounging on my dorm room bed together for texting one another our innermost thoughts could never begin to damage what exists between us.

We have come so far... This is the message in his eyes as he moves in and out of me relentlessly, time and again. "I've protected you and saved you, Jase. And you've done the same for me."

"This is true." He likes it when I answer him aloud. "You're my hero, and I'm always gonna worship you."

It's clear that he appreciates my response; I can see him blush through his beard. "I wanna try and come at the same time. When you see what's in my eyes, you'll understand why I won't let you look away."

He knows my body, as I know his, so it's no surprise to either of us when our mutual orgasm begins. It's intense and so sweet, but I'm not even slightly tempted to close my eyes. Instead, I bite down on my lip when I'd normally tell him I belong to him, and see what is meant for only my eyes.

My hero... These words surge through my mind when I see the way he looks at me. And it's unforgettable.

From the new expression in his eyes, I think I might be his hero, too.

About the Author

Mia Kerick is the mother of four exceptional children—one in law school, another a professional dancer, a third studying at Mia's alma mater, Boston College, and her lone son, finally heading to college. She has published more than twenty books of LGBTQ romance when not editing National Honor Society essays, offering opinions on college and law school applications, helping to create dance bios, and reviewing scholarship essays. Her husband of twenty-five years has been told by many that he has the patience of Job, but don't ask Mia about this, as it's a sensitive subject.

Mia focuses her stories on the emotional growth of troubled people in complex relationships. She has a great affinity for the tortured hero in literature, and as a teen, Mia filled spiral-bound notebooks with tales of tortured heroes and stuffed them under her mattress for safekeeping. She is thankful to NineStar Press for providing her with an alternate place to stash her stories.

Her books have been featured in *Kirkus Reviews* magazine, and have won Rainbow Awards for Best Transgender Contemporary Romance and Best YA Lesbian Fiction, a Reader Views' Book by Book Publicity Literary Award, the Jack Eadon Award for Best Book in Contemporary Drama, an Indie Fab Award, and a Royal Dragonfly Award for Cultural Diversity, among other awards.

Mia Kerick is a social liberal and cheers for each and every victory made in the name of human rights. Her only major regret: never having taken typing or computer class in school, destining her to a life consumed with two-fingered pecking and constant prayer to the Gods of Technology. Contact Mia at miakerick@gmail.com or visit at www.miakerickya.com to see what is going on in Mia's world.

Email: miakerick@gmail.com

Facebook: www.facebook.com/mia.kerick

Twitter: @MiaKerick

Website: www.miakerickya.com

Instagram: @mia_kerick_author

Other books by this author

Love Spell

Coming Soon from Mia Kerick

Scarred

Even in paradise, beautiful faces can hide scarred souls.

ONE tropical island.

Placida Island's gentle ocean breezes and rolling surf beckon to those who wish to reside in remote tropical serenity.

TWO men living in self-imposed exile.

Wearing twisted ropes of mutilated skin on his back and carrying devastating damage in his soul from severe childhood abuse, Matthew North lives alone in a rustic cabin on the shore, avoiding human contact.

Gender fluidity his perceived "crime" against family and friends, Vedie Wilson flees his childhood home so he can freely express his identity.

THREE persecutors seeking their warped view of justice.

Vedie's past refuses to stay in the faraway city he left behind when family members, intent on forcing him to change, threaten the precious peace he's found.

TOO MANY scars to count.

Their beautiful faces masking deeply scarred souls, Matt and Vedie live in hiding from the world and each other.

Can they unite and embrace each other's painful pasts, leaving the scars behind, to find love?

Also Available from NineStar Press

Connect with NineStar Press

Website: NineStarPress.com

Facebook: NineStarPress

Facebook Reader Group: NineStarNiche

Twitter: @ninestarpress

Tumblr: NineStarPress